Way Down South

Stories from the Heart of Dixie

Cover illustration by Jann Sikkink
Cover design by Jodie Vance, Downtown Productions, Inc.

ISBN 0-9728408-0-X

Printed in the United States of America

www.moonstruckpress.com

Dedication

To our mothers and grandmothers and aunts, charter members of the Society Of Women Who Do What Needs To Be Done. And to our fathers, grandfathers and uncles, for whom being Southern was reason enough for existence.

Acknowledgements

Thanks to the members of our critique groups who read our work in its early stages, offered helpful suggestions and spurred us on. Special thanks to Debra Dixon for her time and generous advice. Our love and gratitude for our children, sisters and others in our families, including those who have passed on, for their encouragement and inspiration. We are especially indebted to our husbands for reading every word and for always believing we could do this.

Way Down South
Stories from the Heart of Dixie

Beverly Williams

Beverly Williams

Nina Salley Hepburn

Nina Salley Hepburn

Moonstruck Press

CONTENTS

+✠+

Sunset Carson at the Forked Deer Hotel

By Nina Salley Hepburn

I was spreading Endust over the tops of all the furniture in my new apartment, while my twelve-year-old grand-daughter, Precious, dug through boxes I hadn't unpacked.

"Who is this man, Grandma? I know it's not Granddaddy."

She held in her hand a silver-framed eight by ten photograph of Sunset Carson. Handsome smiling Sunset, wearing a black shirt with yellow bandana tied rakishly around his neck and white cowboy hat. The hat with its upturned brim gave him a certain debonair look for a cowboy, and my heart raced a little even after all these years.

"No, it's not your granddaddy. That's Sunset Carson, a movie star. He came to Dyersburg many years ago."

"It says 'to Josephine, the prettiest girl in Dyer County, love Sunset.' Is that you, Grandma?"

I knew what she was thinking. How could that hand-some young man have ever thought this old woman was the prettiest girl in the county?

"Yes, honey. But that's not the whole story. You see, I was just a girl—a little older than you—and I made a bet with two of my girl friends. I won."

"What was the bet? What did you win? Did you sleep with him?"

"Precious! Hush your mouth." Kids today. Where do they get these ideas? "Of course not. We didn't do such things back then."

"Well, what did you do?"

What did we do? I held the picture close to me, casually wiped it with the Endust-soaked rag. My own wrinkled reflection was superimposed over Sunset's young face. Lord, it was a long time ago.

"I thought I was in love with him." I laughed out loud. "Honey, I didn't even know what love was all about.

"He was the best looking man I'd ever seen and of course he was bigger than life—up there on the screen. I saw every movie he ever made. My daddy had a little picture show business—he showed black and white movies at the schools out in the country. I went with him and helped out during the summer. You remember, I've told you about that. Anyway, everybody loved Sunset Carson. He was always the good guy. Sometimes he played the part of an outlaw—undercover, you see. It was so exciting waiting for him to come out in the open and capture all the bad guys. The whole audience would cheer."

"Gosh, you were so lucky. I wish I got to do something like that." She got a wistful look in her eyes. "But how did he know you?"

"I'm getting to that, Precious. Be patient." I realized that I was still clinging to that picture, still polishing it. "Let's go to the kitchen and have a glass of lemonade."

She rushed ahead of me—slow that I am.

"And some cookies?" she asked. Before I could say a word, she had opened the cookie jar and helped herself.

"Well, darlin', why don't you have some cookies?" I laughed and she did too.

"Tell me the rest of the story. This is so good! I can't wait to tell my friends."

"Oh, honey, it's not that big a deal."

Up until now, it had been my private story. I wasn't sure I wanted it spread all over town. I poured store-bought lemonade into two glasses and set them on the table. I used to squeeze the lemons and make my own, but somehow, it seems like a whole lot of trouble nowadays.

"You don't want to go telling my life story. Besides, nobody cares about an old granny's story.

"I think we've done enough work for today," I said. "Why don't we drive over to Blockbuster and rent a movie? Whatever you want. As long as it's decent for a young girl."

"I'd rather hear about you and Sunset Carson."

Nothing would do but to tell her everything. "But this is our secret—just between you and me," I reminded her.

It was back in the forties, after WW II had ended. There was no television back then. We had to find our own fun. Of course, we listened to stories on the radio. "Inner Sanctum," "The Shadow," "Gildersleeve," things like that. But the thing we loved most was going to movies on Saturday afternoon. They charged us ten cents until we turned twelve; then it was twenty-five cents.

That Saturday afternoon I saw the poster in the lobby of the Frances Theatre. I could hardly believe it. Who would have thought a famous movie star—my favorite star at that— would come to our town? Dyersburg was a really small town back then, very different from the way it is now.

"Look—it's Sunset Carson," I told Mary Jane and Casey. "He'll be here next weekend!"

"I don't like cowboys much," Mary Jane said, sounding like she got the chance to see a movie star every other week.

"Me neither." Casey always agreed with whatever Mary Jane said.

"But he's very handsome," I said. "I've seen all his movies and I'm coming to see him." I didn't tell them how crazy I was about him, that I could hardly breathe for thinking about actually seeing him. I had never in my life seen anybody important in person.

Somehow my daddy found out that Sunset was due in town on Friday and that he was to stay at the Forked Deer Hotel. The hotel's gone now—burned to the ground back in the sixties—but back then it was fine. Right downtown catty-corner from the courthouse, next door to the Frances. Daddy didn't have the slightest idea what I would do with that information. But the wheels started turning in my head and by the time school was out on Friday, I had a plan.

Mary Jane, Casey and I walked out of history class. They started toward Cherry Street, but I stopped them.

"I'm not going home right now," I said. "I'm going downtown." I was dressed for it too. I wore my favorite pleated skirt. Since I didn't have hips back then, I didn't look like I was wearing a plaid whiskey barrel. My sweater matched the skirt, the same shade of red that was in the plaid, and I slipped on a white collar we called a dickey. I had new penny loafers and white socks. My confidence soared.

They looked at me in amazement. We always walked straight home.

"Your mother's gonna be mad," Mary Jane said.

"Yeah," Casey said. "And anyway, why are you going downtown?"

"To see Sunset Carson."

"I thought that was tomorrow. And who cares anyway?"

Mary Jane looked at me like I was crazy. "Come on, Casey, let Josephine do what she wants."

"Wait." Casey turned to me. "Where's he gonna be?"

"At the Forked Deer Hotel," I said. "I'm gonna get his autograph."

"I'm coming with you." Casey surprised me—asserting her independence from Mary Jane.

"Well, let's go." We turned back toward town—the three of us—crunching newly fallen dry leaves on the sidewalk as we walked. We were the Three Musketeers. If one of us did something wild, we all did. Like when we smoked cigarettes in Casey's garage. Her parents made it easy. They both smoked and her mom worked. They left cigarettes lying around the house, so it was easy to get them. They tasted terrible and I almost choked the first time. It was a bad thing to do and when we got caught, my daddy was mad! He grounded me for a whole month.

Mary Jane still wasn't convinced that this trip made any sense. "Tell me, how do you expect to get in his room?"

"I'll tell him my daddy shows all his movies and he'll let me come in."

"He won't care," she said. "Movie stars don't even open their own doors. I'll bet you a dollar you won't get to see him."

"Me, too," Casey said.

"Well, I will." I was determined. At that moment I decided I'd do whatever I had to—even if it meant staying all night. Sooner or later he'd leave his room. If he wouldn't come to the door, I would wait for him.

"You all don't have to come with me, you know. I'll get his autograph to prove it."

"How would we know it was really his?" Shrewd Mary Jane, never trusted anybody. "We'll come with you."

I'd never been in a hotel before. Why would I have? We'd never been anywhere out of town except to visit relatives. The Forked Deer was a dark forbidding place, with old wood and high ceilings. It smelled like musty old books. The lobby furniture looked like something from a Charlie Chan movie. The desk clerk could have had a part in the movie. Round face with wire rimmed glasses and greasy hair that wouldn't quite lie down. Kind of a Peter Lorre look.

"Can I help you, little ladies?" he asked when I stopped at the desk.

"Yes," I said, mustering all my fake confidence. "We're looking for Sunset Carson's room."

"Oh, I'm so sorry." He grinned like he was just tickled to death to turn me down. "Mr. Carson does not wish to be disturbed."

"But Josephine practically knows him," Mary Jane said, laughing. "She's seen all his movies."

I grabbed her braid and yanked it 'til she yelled. "Come on," I said. "There's more than one way to skin this cat. We'll just have to do it the hard way.

"Now, here's what we'll do. First let's casually walk upstairs, then Mary Jane, you start at one end and Casey at the other. I'll take the middle. We'll knock on every door and ask for Sunset. Whoever gets him, call for the others."

"This is not going to work," Mary Jane said. She blew a bubble with her Double Bubble and popped it. "We might as well leave now."

"Shhh. Don't attract attention to us. It'll work. You'll see."

"Yeah, yeah, I know. You've seen all his movies, so you know all about him."

"We don't even know he's on this floor," Casey said as we reached the top of the stairs.

"If he's not, we'll try the third floor. Now let's get started." The hall was wide and kind of dim with medium beige walls, dark brown carpeting and wall sconces the only light. Almost half the tiny bulbs were either missing or burned out.

I heard the echo of fists knocking on wood as I started at the door closest to the elevator. I had my speech all ready. When a voice inside yelled "yeah," I announced that I was looking for Sunset Carson.

"Wrong room," the muffled voice answered.

When I moved on to the next one, I hit the jackpot. A young male voice asked who was there.

"Josephine Cullen," I said. Then I heard voices but I couldn't understand the words. I was so nervous my mouth went dry. I still remember that feeling. I was about to meet my idol—the man of my dreams!

"Sunset says he doesn't know who you are. What's your business?" The voice spoke through the closed door.

He must have thought I was a grown-up, that I had some legitimate reason for being there. "I'm with Cullen Theatres and I want to interview Mr. Carson." I was shaking but I tried to sound genuine.

The door cracked open and I saw a boy's face in the opening. He looked about my age and I thought he was pretty cute, but of course nothing like Sunset Carson.

"You're just a kid," he said. "Mr. Carson is taking a nap and he doesn't want to be disturbed." With that, he reached through the crack and hung a "do not disturb" sign on the knob.

That's when I realized that I knew who he was. He was the freckle faced redhead in my math class. "Hey, I know you," I said. "You're ... you're ..." I couldn't remember his name. I hoped he'd say it.

He didn't. "Yeah, you're in my math class. Now, go on off. He's resting."

I put my foot in the opening. By that time Mary Jane and Casey had come up behind me. "You don't understand," I said. "My daddy shows Sunset Carson pictures all the time. I just want to meet him. I won't cause any trouble."

"He must know Josephine," Mary Jane said. "She's seen all his movies." She laughed out loud and Casey did too.

"You girls better be quiet." The boy held his finger to his lips. "You're gonna get in trouble. You'd better leave."

About that time all hell broke loose. Two policemen appeared out of nowhere. "Are you girls causing trouble?" the burly one asked. "You know you don't belong here in this hotel. Does your mama and your daddy know where you are?"

"They don't care," I said. They would have been furious.

"Who is your daddy?"

I told him and then he asked Mary Jane and Casey.

"We were just about to leave," Mary Jane said.

"Yeah," Casey said.

I wondered who had called them. The boy in the doorway looked puzzled. It couldn't have been him. I thought about Sunset. Was he really taking a nap or had he been on the phone calling the cops on us. I looked at "Red." He shrugged and the look on his face told me he was sorry.

"You girls ought to be ashamed—down here chasing after a visitor to our city." The thinner man smiled at the boy. "Mr. Carson want to press charges?"

"Naw, it's okay." He had come out into the hall and let the door close behind him.

Press charges? Suddenly I felt like this was serious.

"Well, we better take these girls home, Sergeant. Don't you think so?"

"We'll leave on our own," I said. "You don't have to take us." I was about to panic thinking about riding home in a police car. My daddy would kill me! "Please just let us go."

"We didn't do anything," Mary Jane said. "Honest. We'll go straight home."

All the way home in the back seat of the patrol car, we begged them not to tell our parents. It was less than a ten minute drive to our neighborhood on Cherry Street, but it seemed to take hours.

"Just let us off at the corner," I said, as we turned onto Cherry from Sampson. "We can walk from here."

The men laughed and proceeded to Mary Jane's house.

"You go on in," the driver said. Mary Jane got out of the car and ran to her front door. We waited out front until she was inside. Casey's house was next. Once again, we waited. The front door was locked and she didn't have a key. She came back to the car and told the policemen she'd have to go to the back door.

"You come through the house and let us see you at the front door. Okay?"

My agony was prolonged. It would be just my luck that my daddy would be mowing the grass. Maybe Mother and the little kids would be out on the front porch. I wouldn't be as lucky as Mary Jane and Casey, who managed to slip in unnoticed.

As it turned out, Daddy had already mowed the front yard and was sitting on the front porch drinking a glass of iced tea, along with Mother and all the kids. When he saw the car stop, he walked over to take charge. I'll never forget the look he gave me. First there was fear in his eyes, then when the policeman told him what it was about the look changed to extreme disappointment.

"Go to your room, Josephine," he said. That was exactly what I wanted to do. Go to my room by myself.

I was grounded for the whole weekend. Plus I had to

write a note to Sunset Carson saying I was sorry for my foolish behavior. Daddy would deliver it to the Forked Deer and leave it at the desk.

I didn't go to the Frances Theatre on Saturday to see Sunset Carson. Instead I stayed in my room and wrote one hundred lines about coming straight home from school. I didn't want to see Mary Jane and Casey ever again. They would tease me unmercifully and also spread the word all over eighth grade. Everyone would know about my stupid crush on Sunset Carson and the silly thing I had done. I would be disgraced.

"But, Grandma, you said you won the bet."

"I did. You see the autograph on the picture. I just didn't get it the way I planned."

Precious clung to every word. I'd never before seen her so interested in anything I said.

"Remember the cute boy who was protecting Sunset? His daddy was the hotel manager—that's how he got the job. Anyway, he felt so bad about the desk clerk calling the police on us that he took matters into his own hands.

"Sunday afternoon, after Sunset's appearance, the boy brought the picture to me—all signed and in that very same frame."

"Wow! That was really sweet. Did you ever see him again?"

"Oh, yes," I said, thinking about the forty years I'd spent with 'Red.' "He'll be home for dinner any minute."

"Grandma, why didn't you tell me?" She had the look of sudden recognition. She touched her long red hair. "You're talking about Granddaddy."

I laughed. "Now you see—I did win—in more ways than one."

—◈◈—

Party Girl

By Beverly Williams

My cousin and I were in the attic bedroom, smoking Virginia Slims. We were only thirteen, but we were already accomplished smokers, having been stealing cigarettes from our parents for years.

The room was one we used as an extra guest room. It was once a maid's room, back when people had maids, and furnished with cast-offs from our grandmother. An old iron bed with a faded chenille bedspread, a battered chest of drawers, a rocking chair, and pictures of relatives and scenes in Greece and Italy, where no one had ever been.

"Have you ever let a boy touch your boobies?" said BabyO. Her name was Ophelia, but everyone called her BabyO.

"No!" We were the same age, but BabyO was light years ahead of me in experience. Always had been.

"I have. I let Johnny Palmer touch mine last week. Just for a minute."

"Did you like it?" I was trying to act blasé.

"Yeah." She grinned. "But not as much as he did. It really got him hot."

"What if he tells the other boys? Aren't you worried about

getting a bad reputation?"

In those days, having a bad reputation was tantamount to social suicide among the girls and a guarantee of popularity with the boys. Sometimes a bad reputation wasn't even deserved. All it took was a little gossip, so a girl had to be very careful.

"I don't care," said BabyO, flicking the ash off her cigarette. "Let 'em say what they want to."

It was true. She really didn't care, whereas I cared desperately. Not that I had much opportunity to besmirch my reputation, anyway. I had never even been kissed and I certainly couldn't imagine any boy wanting to touch my tiny boobies.

I adored my cousin BabyO and was jealous of her at the same time. All the girls were. She was a beautiful blonde with a dazzling smile that could turn into an adorable pout when she was unhappy. Everything was effortless for her, which was a good thing, because she was also very lazy. She would have been a shoo-in for cheerleader, but she wouldn't even try out, because it was too much work.

"I don't like getting sweaty," she said.

I practiced incessantly and thought I was pretty good, but I didn't even make the squad. Mrs. Jenkins, the gym teacher who picked the cheerleaders, said the key was not popularity, but how good you were. Yeah, right. Like there were ever any dorks who got to be cheerleaders.

When we graduated, I was valedictorian and BabyO was somewhere in the middle. She was smart, but she refused to study. She could have actually learned something in the time she spent copying my homework. She had a good score on the ACT, though, and had no trouble getting into Ole Miss. She wanted me to come with her, so we could be roommates.

"Please, Annie," she begged. "It'll be so much fun. Besides, what if I get stuck with someone who won't like me? You know how mean girls can be."

I was tempted, but I had a scholarship to Vanderbilt, and Ole Miss was just too close to home. Much as I loved BabyO, I wanted to get out from her shadow and spread my wings.

I spent a couple of weekends down at Ole Miss with BabyO. She had become a party girl deluxe, which was no surprise. Out from under the watchful eye of her parents, she was drinking up a storm and experimenting with drugs. She studied just enough to squeak by and practically lived at the Phi Delt house. I tried to talk some sense into her.

"Listen, BabyO, this is not high school. They don't have to keep you here. What will you do if you flunk out?"

"I'm not going to flunk out," she said incredulously, as if the thought had never occurred to her.

But by second semester, she was on probation. She had a burst of ambition and was making good enough grades to get off, but then she fell in love with a football phenom from Yazoo City. She gave up her virginity to him (I was astounded that, at nineteen, she still had it), and they were a big item on the campus for a while. But then he dumped her, which was a first for BabyO. She crashed and burned. It was like she didn't even care if she lived. I was really worried about her and ran up a huge phone bill calling her every night to make sure she didn't commit suicide.

I should have known better. BabyO was like a cat in her resilience. After a month, she bounced back, fur sleek and on the prowl. With flunking out on the horizon, she developed an alternate plan. Even though she appeared to float through life, BabyO was far more calculating than most people realized. By the end of the spring semester, she was pinned, and before the summer was out, she was sporting a big engagement ring. The wedding was planned for Christmas break.

BabyO and Carter Eastman seemed on the surface to be an unlikely couple. To be honest, I wouldn't have picked him myself and I had a far smaller man pool to choose from than BabyO. Carter was a serious, rather owlish-looking law student and BabyO rarely read anything more erudite than Vogue or Town and Country. What they had in common was his family's money. The Eastmans had huge land holdings in the Delta and Carter was an only child. What could be more perfect?

BabyO threw herself into wedding plans with the kind of energy she'd never exhibited for anything else. If they gave degrees for wedding planning, she would have graduated summa cum laude. The whole thing was perfect. She got to spend every weekend at Ole Miss with Carter, and all week planning the wedding. She developed organizational skills worthy of a CEO. No detail was too small to be seen to, to be honed and polished till it was perfect.

Even though everyone thought BabyO was marrying Carter for his money and his family's social position, she actually seemed to love him. I pinned her down one day, because I just didn't want her to make a huge mistake. It was August and we were sitting on her screened porch, drinking iced tea and looking at bridesmaid's dresses in Bride's magazine.

"Are you sure?" I said. "Because you don't have to get married, you know. You can enroll at a junior college to get your grades up and then go back to Ole Miss. Or you could get a job."

"Ha!" she snorted. "Look, I know everyone thinks I'm just getting married because I don't have anything else to do. But I love Carter. I really do. He's sweet and smart but he doesn't think I'm dumb and ..." She looked on the verge of tears.

"You're not dumb, BabyO!" I cried loyally. "You're just not into studying."

She hugged me.

"You know, Annie, I may not be much of a student myself, but I like smart guys. They're usually funny and they're sexy. Like Max."

I was inordinately pleased that BabyO thought my boyfriend was sexy. We clinked our iced tea glasses in a toast.

The wedding was perfect. I was the maid of honor, of course, and there were eight bridesmaids. Believe me, coming up with dresses that flattered nine women was a monumental task, but BabyO pulled it off. She could have been a diplomat. Well, there was one, Carter's cousin from Hattiesburg, who thought the dress made her look fat, but the truth was, she was fat, and there's a limit to what you can do when you don't have much to work with.

I believed BabyO when she told me she was in love with Carter, but I was still worried about the long-term prospects for the marriage. For her, love had always been a temporary emotion. She'd never stuck to anything in her life. What would happen when the new wore off and the inevitable hard times came? She was going to be stuck in small town Mississippi, where the living might be easy, but it's also slow and sometimes stiflingly boring. BabyO couldn't even cook, and there was precious little take-out in their town. Would she be content with church and ladies' bridge parties and tennis? Could a party girl become a housewife?

It was a few months after the wedding, when I was on Spring Break, when I next saw her. She was cheerful and said everything was wonderful, but something didn't seem quite right. She seemed nervous and edgy, and I didn't see the signs of affection between her and Carter that you'd expect of newlyweds.

"Everything okay?" I had to ask, when we were alone.

"Sure," she said, but I wasn't convinced.

"You can tell me, BabyO," I said. "I mean, if you just want to talk."

"Nothing to tell," she said, in that flat tone of voice that means something's wrong, but I'm not going to tell you. "Everything's great. Fantastic."

Well, I worried about her, but what could I do? I had exams and term papers coming up and a boyfriend of my own. BabyO would have to solve her own problems. Then one night I called her house and Carter answered. He said BabyO wasn't there. When I asked when I should call back, he said he didn't know. He sounded like he'd been drinking, so I didn't press it.

I called back the next day, and the live-in maid answered.

"She's gone up to Memphis," she said. "Said she needed to spend some time with her mama."

I thought that was a little strange. BabyO generally spent as little time with her mother as possible. Aunt Pauline is a humorless woman who can best be described as austere. She is an avowed feminist who teaches Shakespeare at the local college. She and BabyO are so different that for years BabyO thought she was adopted and I'm sure Aunt Pauline wondered if there'd been a mix-up in the hospital. She was obviously embarrassed at her daughter's lack of intellect. BabyO's beauty and sunny disposition seemed to count for nothing.

Of course, I imagined all sort of things, including the possibility that BabyO was having an affair. But it turned out that she was only pregnant. She had a difficult pregnancy, with morning sickness and swollen ankles and a weight gain of about fifty pounds. The baby was a girl, and she was beautiful. BabyO turned out to be, if not a perfect mother, at least a better one than anyone expected. She exercised like a fiend to get the weight off, and soon she was playing tennis again. She and Carter spent two weeks in the Caymans on a second honeymoon. I stopped worrying about her.

When I got married, she was my matron of honor. She'd had another baby by then, a little boy, but she looked far from matronly. She outshone all the other girls in the wedding. She'd helped plan the wedding and had talked me into bridesmaids' dresses that were more flattering to her than to anyone else.

For the next couple of years, we rocked along, in the mindless way you do in your twenties, each busy with our own lives. Max and I were in Memphis and BabyO and Carter were in Mississippi. We'd see each other fairly often, at football games and family holiday dinners, but BabyO and I didn't spend much time alone together. I had my career and BabyO had Carter and the children.

Then one summer afternoon I came home from work to find BabyO's BMW convertible parked in my driveway. She was sitting on the screened porch, smoking a cigarette and idly leafing through last month's Southern Living.

"BabyO!" I hugged her. "What are you doing here? Why didn't you call me?"

"I figured you'd be home pretty soon," she said.

"Have you been shopping? God, it's hot out here. You must be parched. Come on in and let me get you some iced tea."

"Could you make that a gin and tonic?"

It was then that I really looked at her. Her usually perfect makeup was about gone. There were only traces of her lipstick left and there were mascara smudges under her eyes. Her face was drawn.

I mixed gin and tonics for both of us and we sat at the kitchen table. I tried to cling to the illusion that this was just an everyday drop-in social visit, even though something told me it was not.

"So," I said brightly, "what's going on? How're the kids? And Carter?"

"They're fine. Everybody's fine. Except me." Her voice was flat, desolate. It wasn't like BabyO to be anything other than cheerful.

A chunk of icy dread formed and lodged in my mid-section.

"What's the matter?"

"They don't know I'm here. I mean, they know I'm in Memphis, but they think I came up here to shop. Oh, God, I didn't buy anything. I have to have something to take back. Maybe I can just say I couldn't find anything. No, Carter'll never believe that. I always find something." She laughed, but it was a mirthless, hollow sound.

"What is it, BabyO?"

"I kept telling Carter something's wrong, but he wouldn't believe me. He said it's all in my head. He just doesn't want to be bothered is what it is. He wants everything to be all perfect, with me there to look good so all his friends will be jealous of him and say how lucky he is."

"BabyO, tell me what's wrong." I was insistent.

"Annie." Her voice choked. "I've got cancer."

"Cancer?" I said stupidly. "You can't. You're too young." I knew better. It was just denial.

"I came last week and they did the tests. I got the results today."

"You came up here by yourself? Why didn't you let me

know? I would have gone with you."

"I know. I didn't think it would be anything bad. I mean, I did but I kept telling myself it was nothing. Carter didn't even know I came. I don't know how I'm going to tell him."

"Good Lord, he's your husband! He's got to know. But, BabyO, you're going to get well. Cancer's curable. And you're young and strong."

"It's cancer of the pancreas, Annie. About the worst kind you can have. You don't get well."

"Well, you're going to," I said, in my most confident, take-charge voice.

It seemed to give BabyO hope, but I was quaking inside. It was all I could do to keep from falling apart. BabyO was more than my cousin. She was my best friend, my sister. I couldn't do without her.

I went with her to tell her parents, then she called Carter and told him she was going to spend the night with Max and me. We didn't even mention her illness again until it was time for her to leave the next morning.

"You are going to be fine, BabyO," I said, but I didn't believe it.

I was even worried about her driving home by herself. Up to now, she'd pretty much floated through life, like a beautiful, irresponsible butterfly. She'd never had to face anything hard, and I frankly didn't think she'd be able to deal with it. I just prayed that Carter would step up to the plate and help her, because I knew she couldn't do it by herself.

For the next couple of weeks, there was a frantic round of consultations and second opinions. I talked to BabyO every day. She seemed to be in a schizophrenic state, sometimes depressed and sometimes unrealistically optimistic, but I was relieved that at least she didn't seem to be suicidal.

Carter took her to Houston to the M. D. Anderson Cancer Institute, but she insisted on having chemotherapy in Memphis, so she'd be closer to the children.

Before she started chemo, I went with her to pick out a wig. I thought it would be a grim occasion, but we had a surprisingly good time, trying on every wig in the store and camping around and giggling like we were children playing dress-up.

I kept up a doggedly optimistic attitude, and Carter did, too. I'd often thought he considered BabyO sort of a trophy, proof to the world that an owlish guy could get a glamorous wife. For an intelligent guy, he was surprisingly shallow. But at least he was hanging in there with her. So far. I hoped he didn't let her down when the illness and the chemo stole her beauty.

When she had her first session of chemo, Carter brought her up to Memphis to Methodist Hospital. She was violently ill, in spite of the anti-nausea medication they mixed in with the lethal chemicals. In between bouts of throwing up, she cried and cursed and swore she wasn't going to do it anymore, but she made it through. Then she insisted on going home.

"I've got to be with the kids," she said. "I don't want them to wonder where I am."

Everyone pretended that was perfectly normal, even though BabyO had a full-time nanny, so she'd be free to play tennis and shop. The children wouldn't have thought it the least bit unusual for her to be gone.

When Max and I went down to Mississippi the next weekend, BabyO was in good spirits.

"The poison's working," she said. "I feel better. Come in here, Annie, I want to show you something."

I followed her into the little studio she'd set up a few

years ago when she'd briefly decided she was going to be an artist. She had some natural talent, but, like most of BabyO's enthusiasms, the artist phase was fleeting, and only the trappings remained. An easel, watercolors, and lots of blank paper.

She handed me a manila folder. In it were delicate little watercolor pictures of two blonde children, sleeping, playing, eating. I knew they were Caroline and little Carter the fourth, even though they didn't look very much like them. There were captions under each one, written in BabyO's swirly handwriting.

Under a picture of a sleeping infant was written, "I couldn't believe you were here at last. What could I have done to deserve such a precious gift from heaven?" I felt tears prick at my eyelids when I realized BabyO was making a memorial to leave her children.

"The drawings are awful, I know," said BabyO apologetically. "Especially the hands. I should have stuck with the art lessons."

"They're good," I said, pasting on my ever-present encouraging smile.

"Damn it, Annie! Stop it! You are the only person I can count on to be honest with me, and ever since I got sick, you've had this nauseating goody two-shoes attitude. I can't stand it! I'm throwing up enough with that poison they're pumping into me. I don't need you making me throw up some more."

"Sorry," I said.

"Now, you tell me the truth. Does that look like little Carter?" She shoved a drawing under my nose.

"No. Actually, it looks like a little frog in short pants."

We dissolved in a fit of laughter, probably more from relief than anything else. I realized how hard it had been for

BabyO keeping up a front for everybody, and I promised to be honest, no matter what. Which I knew was going to be real hard, considering the prognosis. We were a stiff upper lip kind of family, not given to displays of emotion. And I found it next to impossible to face the possibility that BabyO might die. Probably would die.

BabyO had always wanted to go to New York for Thanksgiving, to shop and see the Macy's parade and the stores decorated, but it had just never worked out. Well, Carter, bless his heart, had put together a huge family trip. Everyone in the family was going. We were all staying at the Plaza Hotel and having Thanksgiving dinner at Tavern on the Green in Central Park. We were doing the touristy things, like seeing the Statue of Liberty and the Rockettes' Christmas show, and he'd even finagled impossible-to-get tickets to the hottest Broadway play.

By that time, BabyO was getting tired pretty easily, so on our sightseeing day, we hired this big white stretch limousine to take us around. Aunt Pauline didn't say anything, but I could tell she thought the limo was tacky, the way she had her mouth set in a thin, straight line. But there were too many of us to travel any other way. BabyO loved the way people stared at us like we were celebrities.

The trip was tinged with sadness, and a little desperation, too, but even so, we all had a really good time. I could tell BabyO was trying to imprint some indelible memories on her children's minds, with the parade and Central Park. Late in the day on Thanksgiving, it started to snow, and by the time we went to dinner, there was a thin blanket covering Central Park. It was like magic, since we rarely got snow at home. I'm not generally given to mystical, sentimental thoughts, but I couldn't help but think maybe God had provided it just for BabyO.

BabyO made it through Christmas, I think by sheer force of will. She left me the portfolio of watercolors and letters to keep for her children.

"I know Carter will get married again, Annie," she'd told me. "And I want him to, I really do. He needs somebody and the children need a mother. But I want you to promise me you won't let them forget me."

I promised. When I hugged her, it broke my heart to feel how fragile her body was.

I have sort of a memorial to BabyO, a collection of pictures that I keep on the old chest of drawers that belonged to our grandmother. There's one of us as little girls, playing in the sand box, then as teenagers at the swimming pool. BabyO dazzling as homecoming queen, stunning as a bride. The one I treasure the most, though, is a snapshot of her sitting on a bench in Central Park, all by herself, the snow falling and the day fading around her. She didn't know I was taking it, so she isn't smiling the brave smile she'd kept on her face throughout the trip. She has the gaunt look of a prison camp survivor, and the incongruous blonde wig is just slightly askew. She's looking out into the distance, heartbreakingly beautiful, facing the unknown with the kind of bravery and dignity no one ever expected of the ultimate party girl.

❧

Wednesdays at Three

By Nina Salley Hepburn

They say it's the little things that get you.

"A person could swallow a camel, and choke on a gnat," my mother used to say. She was all the time quoting the Bible like that.

And it was one of those little things that set me off. I don't know why. He had done the same thing maybe a thousand times before. But that day was different ...

The magnolia tree in the side yard near the kitchen was just busting out with plump white blossoms. The soft sweet scent drifted in with the breeze that floated through the open window and mingled with the greasy smell of chicken frying on the stove.

I was inhaling it all and thinking what a nice day it was when Billy swaggered in through the back door like he always did, letting the screen door slam behind him.

"Hot as hell in here," he said. He unbuttoned his shirt, pulled it off, rolled it up in a ball and threw it across the room; took a beer from the fridge, popped the top, pulled out a chair, sat down with feet propped on the table, and swigged half the contents of the bottle. These things he did in one continuous motion.

Next he slammed the bottle on the table, rocked back on the rear legs of the chair, rubbed his round hairy belly, opened his mouth, and belched three times.

Silently, I counted. *One. Two. Three.* And waited. I turned the chicken. It spewed and popped.

He then finished off the beer in one big gulp and repeated the previous performance. Rock back. Rub belly. Belch. Belch. Belch.

One. Two. Three. I turned the gas down, put the lid on the frying pan and walked into the bedroom.

From the top drawer of the bureau, I took the gun. I knew it was loaded, though I had never used it—never even touched it. He always said there was no use in having a gun in the house if it wasn't loaded. The steel felt cold and hard. I was shaking. I held the gun in both hands. My heart raced.

By the time I got back to the kitchen, he had opened and started the second beer, the empty first bottle sitting on the table, waiting for me to throw in the trash. The setting sun behind him cast him in shadow. I could barely see his face. The chicken simmered and sputtered on the stove. A thin path of steam rose from the skillet.

I held the gun so tight it hurt my hands. It was warm now and I was warm all over, like I had a fever. There was a pounding in my chest, a roar in my ears. I aimed the barrel right at his belly.

When Billy saw me pointing the gun at him he put out his hand, his palm flat toward me. His black eyes flashed. "Aw, naw," he said. "God—damn!"

The thought came into my head that I might miss, but there wasn't time to think. Fear took control of my body. I squeezed the trigger. Pop.

"Aaaargh." The sound came from deep inside him. Blood spurted.

I squeezed again. Pop. More blood. And again. Pop, pop, pop, pop. Click, click.

There was blood everywhere—on the walls, on the table, on the window screen—everywhere. It puddled on the kitchen floor, and ran like a stream toward the lowest point near the sink. Smoke filled the room. The stench of gun powder invaded my nostrils, blocking out the magnolia and chicken smells. I dropped the gun. It landed in a bloody pool. Thud. Splatter. My body was shaking. I felt clammy. The house was quiet, except for the soft simmering of the chicken on the stove.

I turned the burner off. I couldn't stand the mess and I felt like I might puke. I took the keys off the hook by the door, got in the car, and drove away.

That was four years ago, but every detail stays with me, like it was yesterday.

Dr. Bitterhaven—he's my shrink—wants me to talk about it. And I do. The others in my group say they're sick of hearing me tell it, but I don't care. Anyway, when I start talking about Billy coming in the door and letting it slam and him popping the top off his beer and throwing his shirt across the room and belching and rubbing his belly, that's when someone always says, *"Here it comes again—belch, belch, belch. Pop, pop, pop."*

Then the rest of them laugh. All except the good-looking sweet-talking shrink who reminds me of my daddy and makes me wish I'd married somebody like him, especially when he smiles at me and winks. Then he says something like, "Now that's enough," and finally they stop laughing. He says if I don't talk about it, how will I ever know what made me do it? So he says to go ahead and tell my story and tells them to be quiet.

And every Wednesday at three o'clock, Big Mama in her starched white uniform comes for me and takes me to the room where we sit in a circle. And when they all get quiet and I know they're listening good, I tell about what happened between me and Billy. They always complain, but what do they know? They're all crazy.

I hear a shuffle now. It's almost three o'clock. And she's shuffling down the hall. *Shuffle, shuffle, shuffle.*

"It's time, Miss Maudie," she says, with that big smile on her face. "Come on. Let's go tell your story again. They're waiting just to hear it." And she laughs—that pig-squealing high-pitch giggle I know so well. *Giggle, giggle, giggle.*

And so we go—Big Mama shuffling and giggling beside me—down the hall to the room where they all wait.

Stranger in the Family

By Beverly Williams

I thought my life was perfect.

Until now. Something has come along to upset everything. There's a new baby in the family. A grandchild, although I'm having a hard time calling him that. It just sticks in my craw.

Before I come across as a hardhearted old curmudgeon or one of those vain men who can't accept the fact that he's grandfather age, let me explain. I was looking forward to being a grandfather. Could hardly wait, in fact. I had visions of cuddly babies, chubby-legged toddlers running across the lawn, adoring adolescents (which might be an oxymoron, but not in my daydreams) coming to me for sage advice. I could picture these fantasy grandchildren; they all looked like Ralph Lauren ads. Handsome, self-assured kids (but well-mannered and polite) wearing their upper-class privilege like expensive tennis togs. They would have clear blue eyes, straight white teeth, and shocks of sun-bleached hair.

But the beautiful babies never came, and so my son Walker and his wife, Caroline, decided to adopt. Which was a disappointment, I'll admit, but one I could live with. Until it turned out that adopting a baby was a long, expensive process which could stretch into years. So now they have brought into our family a child who is a foreigner. A Korean. I am sorry, but I just cannot feel that a Korean baby is a grandchild of mine.

Ellen, my wife, is furious with me. This whole situation has caused a huge rift between us. She says she can't understand me, and I frankly don't understand her, either. And it seems we never will because now we're barely speaking to each other.

She actually encouraged Walker and Caroline in this insane project. Constantly communicated with them by telephone and e-mail. Oohed and aahed over pictures of slanty-eyed infants. It was more than I could stand.

Finally they got word that they had a baby. A boy, six months old. It was Ellen's cue to start a shopping marathon. She has bought the kid more clothes than he'll ever be able to wear.

"Look, honey," she'd say, "isn't this darling? It may be a little big at first, but he'll grow into it."

"Yeah, sure," I'd say, barely glancing at it. I knew I was acting like a jerk, but I couldn't help it. I felt cheated. I was hurt and disappointed, and I didn't feel like pretending anything different.

After a while, she quit showing me the stuff she was buying. The sacks and boxes would come into the house and disappear into what used to be her sewing room. It's now become a room for the baby, for when they come to visit. You'd think the kid was royalty.

Jake is what they've decided to name him. I can't imagine a Korean baby looking like a Jake, but at least they're not naming him after me.

Walker and Caroline picked him up at LaGuardia airport four days ago. They spent the night at a New York hotel and then flew home to Nashville. They wanted to have him to themselves for a week so that they could "bond," but Ellen and

Peggy, Caroline's mother, have just about pestered the life out of them, so the three of us are driving up to Nashville for the weekend. Caroline's parents were divorced and then her father died last year, so I'm the designated driver.

"You don't have to go if you don't want to," huffed Ellen. "Peggy and I can manage perfectly well on our own."

"Don't be silly. Of course I'm going." I've tried to hide my disappointment about the Korean baby, but I think they sense it. Walker and I have always been close and I don't want anything coming between us.

"Well, maybe you shouldn't. If you're not going to act like a grandfather."

I felt like Ellen was trying to shut me out. I was not going to let her get away with it.

"I'm going."

"Fine."

The three-hour trip from Memphis to Nashville was uneventful. Ellen spent the whole time leaning over the seat, chattering to Peggy in the back seat. She included me in the conversation just often enough to keep Peggy from suspecting we were barely speaking. Ellen and Peggy have been friends for years, from even before our children married, but I could see they were already jockeying for position when it came to the baby. Silliest thing I've ever heard of. I sure wouldn't want to be the one to decide which of them got to hold him first.

We were all staying in a nearby motel. I wanted to get checked in first, but the women insisted on going straight to Walker and Caroline's. Let the games begin, I thought to myself.

The two of them raced up the sidewalk to the house as soon as I stopped the car. I unloaded all the stuff they'd brought and made the first trip inside. Walker came out to greet me.

"Hey, Dad," he said, grabbing me in the half-handshake, half-hug we've adopted in recent years. "I'm glad you came."

"Wouldn't have missed it," I said heartily.

"Well, Mom said ..." he began. Then, "I'm just glad you're here." He gave me that shy smile of his and I could see the boy still inside him. I wanted another one like him, that's all. I didn't think it was too much to ask.

"How's it going?" I said. My noncommittal, all-purpose question.

"Great," he said. "Perfect. It's like Jake knew us the minute he saw us. Here he was, all exhausted from that long plane ride, and he didn't even cry. When the escort handed him to Caroline, he just cuddled up to her, like he knew she was his mom."

"I bet he did," I said. I was trying hard, even though it all sounded like a Hallmark card to me. I'm not a sentimental person, never have been.

"I know you don't believe it, Dad, but if you'd seen it ... we've already got a bunch of pictures. I'll show you the one when Caroline first holds him, and you can tell."

"Here, son, take this contraption your mother bought," I said, to get us out of greeting card mode. I handed him a box. "Supposed to make ... Jake into some kind of superbaby." It was the first time I'd referred to him by name.

"They told us he might have a hard time adjusting," said Walker. "But he's been perfect. He's slept right through the night ever since we've had him. It's like he knows he's home."

"How's the dog like him?" I asked.

We used to have this Korean guy who delivered for the dry cleaner. Our old Irish Setter hated him. For no apparent reason. I was afraid Walker's dog Hoodlum might have the same kind of prejudices.

"Man, Hoodlum loves him. Looked at Jake kind of suspiciously at first, but now he tries to lick him. It's really cute."

Okay, so I was the only one with prejudices.

We came in the house and I could hear the women chirping away like a bunch of mother birds. Poor kid, I thought.

"Come on in and see him, Dad," said Walker.

I followed him down the hall to the royal nursery. Everything matching, every inch decorated. Honest to God, how people can expend so much effort on one little kid who's not even going to notice. But I'm not saying a word. Once your children get married, they don't want your advice any more. If they ever did.

Peggy was sitting in the rocking chair holding him, while Ellen hovered over her, her fingers twitching. I could tell she could hardly wait to get her hands on him. Ellen said it was tradition that the girl's mother had first dibs on the baby. But after that, all bets were off. Knowing Ellen, she privately intended to become the favorite grandmother. More power to her, if that's what made her happy. I was content with my role as grandmother consort. I would do what was required, but nobody could make me feel it.

He was kind of cute, though, cuter than his pictures. Jake. I was going to have to practice calling him by name.

"Hey, boy," I said, then realized I sounded like I was talking to Hoodlum. I leaned down and smiled at him. He immediately screwed up his face and let out a howl. His already-tiny eyes disappeared and his face turned dark red. Everyone looked at me like I'd done something wrong. Hell, it wasn't my fault, but I felt embarrassed anyway. Actually, kids usually liked me. But obviously not this one.

"He's just not used to you, Dad," said Walker, scooping him up with a practiced motion. How had he learned that in less than a week? The baby gradually quieted down as Walker held him on his shoulder, unabashedly kissing him on the head. The dueling grandmothers started cooing and chirping again, and the baby smiled. I pretended to examine a Humpty Dumpty lamp sitting on top of a chest.

Then Walker brought him over to me.

"This is your granddaddy, Jake," he said to the baby, as seriously as if he believed the kid understood what he was saying. Maybe he did, because the howling began again.

"Look," I said, "I think this is too much for him. I'm going outside for a cigarette." You can't smoke in Walker and Caroline's house.

As I walked down the hall, I heard the kid's howling subside. I think everybody was glad I was gone. I felt like I'd been kicked out of my own family. Here I'd been thinking this foreign baby was the intruder, and now it seemed like it was me. Displaced by a bad-tempered, slanty-eyed infant. I felt an ache, an almost physical yearning for the blue-eyed grandchildren of my dreams.

I smoked a cigarette, then wandered around the back yard. Walker and Caroline bought this wonderful house in an older part of Nashville, a testament to his success as a lawyer and some astute investments. Caroline had just quit her high-powered job in a public relations firm to be a stay-at-home mother. Which I did approve of, by the way.

After a while, Walker came out to make sure my feelings weren't hurt.

"Jake just needs to get used to you, Dad," he said.

"I know," I said, though I had my doubts. I petted Hoodlum, who liked me just fine.

They finally wore the baby out and put him down for a nap. We all went in the den for drinks before dinner. I was looking forward to some adult conversation, but it was all about Jake. It was pretty damn boring, but the rest of them seemed fascinated. Even Walker. I looked longingly at the new Forbes magazine on the coffee table, but I knew if I picked it up, I could count on a lecture on rudeness from Ellen. Besides, I didn't want to hurt Walker and Caroline's feelings.

Then Walker went into his study to return a phone call from a client and the women gravitated to the kitchen to fix dinner. I skimmed the Forbes, then wandered down the hall to the bathroom. As I came out, I glanced into the baby's room. I could see a little leg kicking in the air above the crib bumper. I edged in quietly and watched him as he watched a cow-jumping-over-the-moon mobile that hung over the crib.

He wasn't crying yet, so I knew he hadn't seen me. I tiptoed further in. At least he looked healthy. The chubby little legs looked strong already. In a few years, they would have him playing soccer. I pictured him running up and down a field in a little uniform. I figured Ellen would want to make a special trip up here every time he had a game.

Then he turned his head and his dark, almost black, eyes looked straight into mine. I braced myself for the howl. He regarded me seriously for a minute, like a solemn little Buddha. Then he smiled! I looked around to see if someone else had slipped into the room. No one. Faint sounds of female conversation still drifted from the kitchen. I smiled back at him and waited cautiously. He kicked his legs and kept on smiling, so I tiptoed closer.

"Hi, Jake," I whispered.

He made a sort of cooing sound. Amazingly, he still didn't cry. So I reached into the crib and touched his hand. I felt the incredible velvet-soft smoothness that only baby skin has. I'd forgotten how it felt. He wrapped his fist around my index finger. With my other hand, I started to play little finger games with him, tiptoeing up his tummy to his chin.

"I'm going to get Jake's chinny-chin-chin," I whispered, feeling a little foolish.

Jake chuckled. I wondered if he'd done it before. Maybe I was the first one who'd made him laugh out loud.

I started to sing some silly songs to him, softly so no one else would hear. He seemed to like them, because he kept cooing and chortling. I decided to take a chance. I picked him up and waited, holding my breath. Instead of the expected howl, he settled onto my shoulder. I felt a little hand on my neck. I'd forgotten how comforting it was to hold a baby.

I walked Jake around the room. I told him confidentially what I thought of all the intense decorating. He cooed in agreement.

"Let's go give them a surprise, Jake," I said. "Don't let me down, now." I hoped he didn't betray me with a sudden howl.

We walked down the hall and stood in the doorway to the kitchen. Then they turned and saw us. Conversation and motion stopped. Tears gathered in Ellen's eyes. Oh, God, it was another Hallmark moment.

"Look who I found," I said, trying to keep things light. To my profound embarrassment, I heard a catch in my voice.

They all started talking at once, making a big deal out of it. But I knew Jake thought it was just as silly as I did. When he got a little older, I'd tell him about how we first got to know each other. Without all the sentimental details, of course.

I looked out the window into the back yard. It was almost dusk now. For a fleeting moment, I could see my blonde grandchildren running across the lawn. Then they smiled, waved goodbye to me and disappeared with the fading day.

Your Mama Loves You

By Nina Salley Hepburn

The shrill ringing of the telephone sliced across the lonely confines of the dismal room. Effie pushed away from the table where she sat waiting for Jeep. He'd been gone more than an hour. Her heart pounded and her feet felt like dead weights. She glared at the nagging instrument.

"All right," she said, breathless, her mouth against the receiver. Her free hand clutched her large bosom and she sank onto the bed beside the telephone. The springs squeaked in protest against her bulky body.

"Is this Ms. Effie McCoy?"

"Speaking." The pounding inside her wouldn't stop, grew louder, like the sea, almost drowning out the voice on the other end of the line.

"Ms. McCoy, this is Sergeant Hanson. We've got a man down here, says he's Jeep McCoy. Says you're his mama."

"That's right, Jeep's my boy." Oh, dear God, she thought. "What's he done?"

"Well, ma'am, it don't look good for him. I think it best you come on down here."

"Is he all right? He ain't hurt, is he?" Louder and louder,

filling her ears. She had to strain to hear the words she didn't want to hear.

"He's all right, but you'd best come on down here."

"I ain't got any way, mister," she said. Why had she let him go? "It's too late for the bus to run."

"This is serious, ma'am. I'll send a car for you. Deputy'll be there in about ten minutes. You be ready?"

"I'm ready now." She dropped the receiver into its cradle, staring for a moment at the ugliness of it. The pounding wouldn't stop. She took the cord in her hand, wound it around her wrist. I could pull it out of the wall, she thought, maybe then it would stop. But just as quickly, she let it go, for she knew the sound was not connected to the plastic device or the wire that was screwed to the wall and then hid somewhere within the innards of the house.

Her eyes turned toward the ceiling and picked out a large triangular section of old yellowed paper that had let go of the plaster. I could glue it back, she thought, if I had a ladder. She eased up from the sagging mattress and shuffled over to the hotplate in the kitchen-corner of the room, poured a cup of coffee from the stained enamel pot. Wincing at the strong bitter taste, she forced it down.

Almost a year they had lived here in this furnished room in Ripley. It had been a good place for them. Jeep had found a job at a gas station two blocks away. She could ride the bus to town to get the few things they needed. The woman who owned the house, Mrs. Blanchard, was a scrawny little thing who flitted around the house and yard, in a lurch, talking to this one and that one. They seemed to be friends—all the roomers and Mrs. Blanchard—but Effie had made it clear from the beginning that she and Jeep would be apart from the rest. She had learned long ago that it was best not to get involved.

Once they had made friends when Jeep was just eighteen and they had lived in a similar room in another town in another state. Effie had worked as a cook in a Mexican restaurant six days a week. Jeep mowed yards during the summer and chopped wood in winter. They became close to Georgia, a young widow who lived in the rooming house with her six year old daughter, Betsy. On Sundays they all rode the bus to the Holiness Evangelical Church.

Georgia expressed concern that Jeep had had no schooling. Often on Sunday afternoons, she would sit at Effie's table, patiently counting out change with Jeep. He delighted in playing the money game. Effie felt a little guilty that she had neither the patience nor the ability to teach Jeep.

"Effie," Georgia said one night on their way home from a movie, "have you ever thought about what will happen to Jeep when you're gone?"

"'Course I have." Effie turned her eyes to the window on the opposite side of the bus, watched the lights of the city rush by. "I've thought about it lots. But I'm just putting it in the hands of the Lord. After all, he give me Jeep to raise. I reckon he'll take care of Jeep when he sees fit to call me."

"Effie, you can't think like that. I agree to put your faith in the Lord, but Jeep needs to be prepared to get a good job, to do something for himself ..."

"I took him to school when he was the age to go, but they wouldn't keep him, said he couldn't learn. I've tried to give him a chance to learn to do handy work. He knows how to run a mower, he can handle an axe good as any man. You know how strong he is."

"But, Effie, he might learn a trade. If he's ever to take care of himself he has to have a trade."

"Who's gonna teach him? You know how slow he is to

learn. Don't nobody have the patience—except you."

Georgia hesitated, then spoke slowly. "There's a school especially for people who—people like Jeep. Over at Benton. He could go there and stay 'til he learned a skill. Then he could come back home with you and get a good job."

"Jeep wouldn't like that, Georgia." Effie shook her head. "A school for retarded. No, Jeep has always been right with me. Why, he probably wouldn't learn a thing just for spite."

"I think you should give it a try," Georgia pleaded. She patted Effie's hand as the bus lurched forward. "You know I love that boy, Effie, like my own brother. I just think it's wrong not to give him a chance."

"I don't want to talk about it no more," Effie said, turning away. She didn't tell Georgia that she'd seen the school at Benton. When Jeep was seven and couldn't stay at the regular school, the teacher had said to take him to the retarded school and Effie had dressed Jeep up in his Sunday best and they rode the bus all the way to Benton. She was prepared to leave Jeep, her only baby, with strangers so they could teach him what she couldn't.

But when the smiling matron with her city-smooth looks and slick black hair led them into the big play room where all the others were and Effie looked around at the misshapen others, then at Jeep's pretty face, pale and tense in wonderment, she squeezed his hand and fled. All the way to the bus stop, they ran together, their fright turning to relief. A feeling of overwhelming joy surged through Effie's very being. She had protected Jeep from a miserable fate.

Together they had escaped. She hugged him tightly, smoothing his blonde hair, now damp around his face. "Mama won't leave you, baby, don't you never worry. Mama will always take care of you."

Effie took another sip of coffee and waited. It was all mixed up together—that trip to Benton, and Georgia and Betsy. And what happened when Jeep was eighteen. God, she thought, how old is he now? Nearly fifty, though he still has the mind of a child, still looks like a child in many ways.

Georgia had taught Jeep to tell time, to read simple words, like stop, walk and don't walk. She took the canned foods from the pantry and lined them up on the table, told him the names, had him repeat them. Then she mixed them up and asked him again. After a few weeks of practice, he could read all the groceries.

"Let me take Jeep shopping with me, Effie," Georgia said after one of the games. "I'll tell him what I want and see if he can pick it out."

"Sure, Georgia. You really have a way with him. Nobody has ever been as good to Jeep as you."

Two days later, Jeep ran into their room, gasping for breath, spilling words that didn't make sense to Effie. "Mama—after me—police—come get Jeep—Georgia hit me …"

Effie was stunned. "What happened, Jeep? Tell Mama what happened."

"Georgia—mad at Jeep—hurt Jeep. Here." He took Effie's hand and placed it on top of his head. Effie felt a lump.

"Jeep, why would Georgia do that? She loves you." Something was terribly wrong, she knew, but what? How could she make Jeep explain?

"Georgia hates Jeep. Hit Jeep with shovel."

"Why, Jeep? Why did Georgia hit you?"

"Betsy cried—I didn't hurt her but she cried. No, Mama, Jeep didn't hurt Betsy."

"Stay here in this room." An anger she had never known

rose in her. "I'll get to the bottom of this." She almost ran down the hall to Georgia's room.

Muffled sobs came from the room and she flung open the door without knocking. "Georgia, what in Jesus' name is Jeep trying to tell me?"

Georgia was sitting on the bed beside the crying child. "Go outside, Effie. I'll be out in a minute."

Effie leaned against the wall in the hall, her heart beating so fast she thought it would cut off her breath. Then Georgia was beside her, pain showing in her face. She wiped away the tears.

"Effie, I found Jeep in the garage with Betsy. He was— touching her, in a way he shouldn't be. I had to call the police."

"The police?" Was that her voice screaming? "You called the police on Jeep? How could you? He wouldn't hurt Betsy. You're wrong."

"I'm sorry, Effie. He had her panties down. He was— holding her down on the floor. Betsy was terrified, begging him to let her go. He just held her there. I had to hit him to make him get up. Effie, I've tried to tell you: he needs to be at Benton!"

The police, Effie thought. Benton. She ran back to their room and threw their few belongings in the two old cardboard suitcases. She and Jeep hid inside the garage next door. They watched through the cracks, saw the police car drive up. Effie's fear controlled her every move and she held Jeep tightly. He laughed quietly at their game. When the police had gone, they walked to the bus station and rode the bus to a new town, a new room. But they didn't make new friends.

Over the years, Effie had thought a lot about Georgia and

Betsy. At first, she wondered if it could be true about Jeep, but when she looked at his innocent face, she didn't believe it—wouldn't believe it. If there had been any truth to it, she decided, their close friendship had probably been the cause. Jeep and Betsy were together too much. There would be no more friends like that. She and Jeep had no need for anybody else.

But Jeep had a need Effie didn't understand, couldn't control. Another town, another child, on the school playground, in the city park, the opportunity would present itself and Jeep would run to her for protection. He was her life, her only reason for living and she couldn't bear to think of him being locked up, either in Benton or in jail. So they ran. To a new room in a new town. She always talked to Jeep about what he had done, told him it was wrong, made him promise never to do it again. She promised herself to watch him closer.

And she tried. But you can't watch a grown man every minute, she thought. Like tonight. He just wanted to walk to the drugstore for a chocolate ice cream cone. Promised to come right home. And now he's caught. She had known it would happen eventually, but she wasn't prepared for it, couldn't be prepared for it.

The pounding, water pounding the shore. It was back, louder than before. Had it ever stopped? But it wasn't the same. She rose slowly, took her coat from a hook on the wall and opened the door.

"I'm Deputy Forsyth, ma'am," the figure in the stiff blue uniform said. "Sargeant Hanson called?"

"Yes, I'm ready to go. Tell me, what's happened to my boy?"

"Well, ma'am, I know this is going to be a shock to you." His hand was at her elbow, supporting her as they walked down the steps into the night chill. "He's raped a little girl, just ten years old. She's in the hospital now. I know this is hard on you, him being retarded and all. But there's no doubt about it. A cruiser was driving along and heard the child scream. Caught him in the act. "Course they'll probably go easy on him—him being retarded and all. It's not like he was responsible, like a normal person. They'll probably send him to Benton …"

Effie wasn't listening anymore. The harsh pounding had slowed to a steady, almost comforting beat. She relaxed, her tired back against the soft cushioned seat of the patrol car. She thought about the days and weeks ahead.

She could almost hear the engine of the Greyhound bus starting up, smell the exhaust fumes, feel the familiar seat beneath her. Her eyes closed, she could see the retarded school up on a hill with trees all around. It didn't seem like such a bad place anymore.

See You in Paradise

By Beverly Williams

A homeless man had set up housekeeping under a bridge not too far from our house. His begging operation was next to a stop sign, and whenever we passed, my husband gave him a dollar or two.

"Thank you, brother," the man always said. "See you in paradise."

"Yeah, sure," I snorted. "He's just going to spend that money on booze."

"So it brings him a little happiness," said Leo, shrugging his shoulders. "Anyway, you don't know who's going to end up in heaven. It might surprise you."

Leo was always a more tolerant person than I am, I have to admit. But I had a hard time believing a scruffy old alcoholic or drug-addicted beggar, who'd done Lord knows what in his sorry life, would end up in my clean, fluffy-clouded heaven. It might have something to do with being raised Baptist, or maybe it was just me. My picture of heaven was pearly gates, gold-paved streets, and angels with wings. I knew my grandmothers and one of my grandfathers were there—I wasn't sure about the other one, who'd been caught embezzling from the bank and committed suicide. And I worried about Aunt Lillian, who'd led a wild, alcohol-infused life that ended when she ran her convertible off the road into a tree.

Leo and I were still young in those days, busy with work and family. We went to church erratically, and I didn't think too much about heaven or hell, either. Still, the phrase had a certain appeal and Leo and I would sometimes say it to each other, usually in a joking sort of way.

Then Leo was diagnosed with lung cancer. He'd stopped smoking years ago, but obviously not soon enough. It was a terrible time, with hospitals and chemo and both of us trying to keep the other's spirits up. At first Leo, who'd rarely even had a cold or a headache, was convinced he would beat it. Finally, though, we had to face the inevitability. The last words he said to me before he slipped into a coma were, "I love you, babe. See you in paradise."

I clung to those words like a talisman. I knew I would miss Leo, but I had no conception of how much. I could see the world going on around me, but I wasn't in it. Like when you put the television on mute. The children propped me up through the funeral, and our friends surrounded me, offering kindness and casseroles. I was vaguely grateful for everyone, but nothing changed the fact that my darling Leo was gone for good.

I missed him with a physical yearning, regretted every minute I hadn't spent with him. Felt guilty about the times I took the children and went to Florida, leaving him to work and manage on his own. Never mind that having the house to himself for a week was probably a vacation in itself. I was mad at him for leaving me and I wanted him back, so I could do things all over again. Do them right this time.

I grieved and grieved and talked about Leo incessantly, rehashing all the old stories from our life together. Leo became funnier and stronger and far more saintly than he had been in real life. I could tell I was becoming a bore by the way my long-suffering friends' eyes began to glaze over and the way they would sneak looks at their watches whenever I fired up another one of our stories. I knew they were getting tired of me. Even my children began to consider me a burden. But I couldn't stop. On and on I droned, often to our dog, Romeo, if no one else was around. He was the dumbest dog we'd ever had, good for virtually nothing, but I have to say this for him, he was an excellent listener.

Finally, the fog of bereavement began to dissipate. The sounds of life started seeping back in and I could taste and feel again. I could enjoy the luxury of a hot bath and the pure sweetness of my little granddaughter's sticky kisses. I read books. I made vegetable soup.

I still missed Leo constantly. I thought about his last words to me. "See you in paradise." Was it possible? Would I see Leo again or was it just a romantic dream? Not true theology but pop religion like that angel craze that was going on. I began going to church every Sunday. I joined a women's Bible study group. They spent a lot of time talking about things other than the Bible, but they were a compatible group nevertheless, and it was comforting to be with believers.

I started working at a homeless shelter a couple of days a week, sort of as a memorial to Leo, and to give me more tolerance. I looked for the man under the bridge, but I never saw him. Gradually my life settled into a structure. I was still lonely but reasonably content.

Then one day I was driving downtown to the homeless shelter, which is not in the best of neighborhoods. I was passing a housing project when a little boy on a bicycle appeared out of nowhere. He was looking over his shoulder, peddling furiously and heading straight for my car. Gripped by horror, I slammed on the brakes and jerked the steering wheel to the right, as he loomed in front of me. My last thought was the nightmare fear that I had killed a child as my car jumped the curb and slammed into the front of a pawn shop.

I can feel my mind stirring, but it feels separate from my body and I don't know where I am. Then I remember the accident, the little boy. I must be in a hospital. I open my eyes, expecting to see a sterile white hospital room, to find myself hooked up to an I.V.

But instead of a hospital room ceiling, there is blue sky above me. I am not in a hospital bed but lying on the grass, on an old quilt my grandmother made, the one we used to take on picnics. I wonder how I got here, but I am not frightened, just puzzled.

I realize I am dreaming, the way you do when even in a dream, you know the situation is too odd to be real. When I look down and see that I am wearing short, faded cut-offs, I know for sure it's a dream. Those old cut-offs have long since been replaced with modest, ironed knee-length shorts.

I sit up and look around. It's a gorgeous summer day, but not hot. A little breeze plays over the bare skin of my tanned arms and there's a faint insect hum and birds chirping. I wonder why I'm alone. Then I feel a cold, wet nudge on my arm and I see a dog. Sam, our old basset hound, the dog we had before Romeo. I give him a hug. But how can this be Sam? He's been dead for years. Leo buried him in the back yard.

I am relieved when I hear someone call my name. I like occasional solitude but not this spooky feeling of aloneness.

"Margaret?" It's my mother. I jump up from the blanket and run to her.

"Mama!" I throw my arms around her.

She is the young mother of my childhood, not the shrunken old lady she was in her last days. She even has on a dress I remember, a sort of garden party dress of pale peach silk that swirls around her slender legs and makes her look even prettier than she is.

"Oh, honey, I'm so glad to see you," she says. "We've all been waiting for you."

"Where are we, Mama? I don't recognize this place."

"Paradise. We're in heaven."

"Oh, Mama," I laugh. This can't be heaven. We're just in a field, not up on a cloud somewhere. There are no pearly gates, no streets of gold.

"I know you think you're dreaming," she says, as if reading my thoughts. "Everyone does at first. But you're not. This is really heaven. You're going to love it here." She reaches down to pet Sam. "Oh, there's Daddy."

My father arrives. "Hey, sweetheart," he says, wrapping me in a bear hug and swirling me off my feet. I catch a whiff of the sweetish pipe tobacco that I always associated with him. "How's my girl?" He's wearing his favorite golf sweater and he looks young, too. Slim.

He kisses my mother on the cheek while keeping an arm around my shoulders. "Is she acclimated yet?"

"Give her time, Jack. You know it takes a while." She turns to me. "When I first got here, I couldn't believe it. I didn't think I deserved to be in heaven, so I was sure I wasn't. I kept waiting to wake up back in that bed in the nursing home. I couldn't believe I was young again, and with my darling Jack at last." She gives him that look they always had between them, special and private.

"Let's walk up to the house," says my father. "The rest of the family is waiting."

We walk up a worn path through the woods, my parents on either side of me. As we come into a clearing, I recognize our old house, the house I grew up in. We sold it after Mama died. I felt so guilty about that, but the neighborhood was changing and our children were happy in the suburbs where we lived.

There on the porch, sitting next to each other in a swing, are my two grandmothers, my mother's mother and my father's mother. They never got along and always avoided each other whenever possible. I nudge my mother and give her a questioning look. She laughs.

"Oh, they've become really good friends. This is heaven, honey. Everyone gets along."

As we get to the porch, all my relatives rush forward, enveloping me in hugs and bestowing kisses and greetings. They are all talking at once, just like they did in life. Someone is carrying a baby that died in infancy. A plethora of family pets from years past frolic around us. It's beginning to seem real, so maybe I am in heaven. I'm relieved to see my grandfather Walter, the embezzler, and my wild Aunt Lillian.

"Walter was admitted on probationary status," whispered Daddy. "He had to do a lot of charity work to make amends."

"What about Aunt Lillian?"

"Oh, she got right in. You get extra points if you die early. To make up for not getting to live out your life on earth. And you get some for having a good heart and a sense of humor. God likes people who don't take themselves too seriously."

The family is beginning to set out a picnic lunch under the oak tree on the lawn. My cousin Phoebe plops one of her marvelous lemon meringue pies on the table.

"You better cover that up," I say.

"Don't have to," says Phoebe. "No flies. No mosquitoes. Only nice insects like butterflies and ladybugs and bees. The bees don't sting, though, only pollinate. And the spiders spin webs, but they don't bite."

It seems like a fantasy, but I no longer feel as if I am dreaming. It feels real. And if it's real, then I have a worry. I am almost afraid to ask.

"Where's Leo?" I say. If Leo isn't here, I don't want to stay.

As soon as I say the words, the music starts. Not harps and violins in a celestial melody, but rock and roll from the fifties. There on the front porch stands Leo, looking like he did the day I met him. Tall and skinny and gorgeous, with his longish hair combed back into an Elvis-style d.a., and a cocky grin on his face. My Leo. He jumps off the porch and bops down the sidewalk toward me as the unseen band plays "Rock Around The Clock." I hurl myself into his arms.

He lifts me off the ground and swings me around. "Maggie, Maggie," he says, covering me with kisses. "I've missed you so much. The only thing wrong with this place was you weren't here."

"Is this really heaven, Leo? It's not a joke or a dream? I dream about you all the time, but I always wake up by myself."

"I promise. I told you I'd see you in paradise."

We wander down the tree-shaded street, holding hands. I realize the arthritis that has been plaguing me lately is gone.

"I had a wreck," I say, as I suddenly remember. "A little boy on a bicycle ... oh, my God!"

"Don't worry, he's okay. He was scared, but not even a scratch, thanks to you. I think now he'll be more careful about riding in the street."

"Oh, Leo, the children," I say. "If I'm dead ..."

"It's sad, honey, but that's life. They're grieving now, but they'll be all right. Up here you learn to let things go. And you can help me watch over them now."

It seems strange to hear a teenage-looking Leo talking with the wisdom of an old man. I reach up and touch his hair. He instinctively pulls back a little, then looks at me and grins. Leo always spent hours on his hair, and he hated for anyone to touch it.

"You look funny with that d.a.," I say, teasing him.

"I think I look great," says Leo. "And you're beautiful. I always loved you in those short cut-offs."

"Oh, Leo," I say, "are we really together again?"

"We really are," he says.

"Where do we live?"

"Wherever you want to. We can live in our old house or we can pick out a new house. We can even live in our first apartment. Remember that?"

I feel my face flush as the memories come flooding back of those early married days in the shabby little garage apartment, where we made love every night and all weekend. We had no money and we were never happier. I wonder if young people today, who have so much so soon, are as happy as we were. A thought occurs to me.

"Leo, do people have sex in heaven?"

"You betcha!" says Leo, with a grin.

On a nearby lawn, I see The Coasters. They are playing "Charlie Brown." Leo grabs my hand and we dance out into the street. It's like we are at a high school dance. I see familiar faces. Darryl Cooperman, who was killed in Viet Nam. Margo Overall, who drowned trying to save her little boy. Mrs. Vincent, my favorite English teacher. They smile and wave.

"Guess we better show up for the party," says Leo. "Since it's in your honor."

We walk back up the street where the family members are milling around the picnic table, beginning to fill their plates.

I see my grandmother Nancy's fried chicken, Aunt Louise's potato salad, my mother's squash casserole. There is a sack of potato chips and a jar of dill pickles provided by Uncle Nate's wife, Naomi, who was a terrible cook and lazy to boot. She was always the subject of much disapproval by the rest of the family, but no one seems to mind up here. Tables and chairs dot the lawn. I recognize all the family, even my grandfather on my mother's side who died before I was born.

Leo and I cruise around the table, heaping our plates.

"I'm just going to have a sliver of lemon pie," I say. "These shorts are kind of snug."

"Have a big piece," says Mama. "You can't get fat here. Although those shorts are a little tight." Some things never change, even in heaven.

At the edge of the crowd, I see someone I don't recognize.

"Alex!" calls Leo. "Over here."

The man walks over. He is dressed in tennis shorts, with a sweater around his shoulders. He is very handsome, sort of Robert Redford-looking, but younger. I give Leo a quizzical look.

"You remember Alex," Leo prompts.

I don't, but apparently he knows me.

"Good to see you, Maggie," he says. There's something about his voice. He smiles at me. How could I not remember someone who looks like that?

"Alex and I play a lot of tennis together," says Leo. "Never have to wait for a court around here."

"I got a little rusty all those years I was living under the bridge. But I'm getting my game back."

I stare at him.

"It's like Alex always said, Maggie," says Leo. "See you in paradise."

Mama's Elvis Story

By Nina Salley Hepburn

You might say it was Mama's legacy to me. The Elvis story was all she had to leave me when she died. That and a 14-year-old Chrysler that leaked oil and wouldn't go into reverse anymore. Plus a yard sale portable typewriter in a beat-up cardboard case.

She pulled me close to her with what little strength she had left and whispered. "Honey—don't let me and Elvis down—sell the story—it's all up to you ... now ... just you." Even with pure oxygen pumping in through her nostrils, she gasped for every breath.

I looked at her pale bony face and her thin gray hair showing only a hint of the red it had once been. Tears filled my eyes and ran down my face as I realized the end was near. She was too far gone to notice.

She coughed hard once, then started to whisper again. I leaned toward her and her cold fingers reached for me.

"I wish—just wish—I had one—more—cigarette—"

With that she gasped and shuddered. Her hand fell to the

bed and I knew she was gone. The cigarettes had finally done her in.

Thus ended a way of life established two years earlier when she entered the Pineview Nursing Home. Each morning I drove to the nursing home and helped with her breakfast, then on to my job as assistant to the president of Robertson Insurance Agency. I spent my lunch hours feeding her between bites of my own sandwich. Then after work, it was back to the nursing home to help with her dinner and stay until bedtime.

I went through the routine of making funeral and burial arrangements, not really thinking about what my life would be like without her.

She had told me she wanted to be buried in West Helena, Arkansas, so that's where I had them take her. We had a small service in the little Presbyterian Church she had attended as a child and buried her in the church cemetery. Her older sister, Betty Jean, who never visited her while she was sick, did come all the way from Florida for the funeral. A few cousins that I had never met and a couple of her old friends from high school came, so it was a respectable funeral. The preacher was young and had never known her, but he said her name, Lula Thompson, right and said nice things about her. I wanted to give a eulogy about the kind of mother she had been but I couldn't seem to come up with the right words so I didn't.

The next week I answered an ad in the paper and sold her car for $150 to a greasy little man who came by with a tow truck. The old Chrysler had sat in my garage for over two years where I'd parked it when Mama had to quit driving. He said he wanted it for parts. I lifted the oil-soaked cardboard from the garage floor and put it in the garbage. Little by little, I was erasing her from my life.

That night, I took the typewriter from the closet in the room where Mama had stayed when she came to live with me. I thought about putting it on the curb for the trash collectors. Who uses a typewriter anymore? Especially an old worn out portable. But I opened the case and fingered the wobbly keys and thought about Mama. Mama sitting at the kitchen table in a tiny walk up, typing her letters, Mama sitting at a desk in a motel when we were on the road. I thought about all the times I woke up to the sound of that typewriter clicking away. I could almost see her now—beautiful like she was, with fluffy red hair and big blue eyes and a smile that made everybody love her. She had a Hollywood type figure and she dressed to show it off.

Thinking of her, I cried until my eyes hurt. I started to close the case. Then I noticed a yellow note pad protruding from the pocket in the top. It was a handwritten list of the people she had contacted to try to sell her story, beginning with The National Enquirer. There were also pages of notes about Elvis and that night. At the top of the first page she had printed in bold letters, ME AND ELVIS.

The memories came flooding back.

We flew out of West Helena in Mama's powder blue Pontiac convertible that August morning. "We're gonna have some fun today," she said as we turned toward the bridge. I knew we would. It was always fun traveling with Mama. She loved that convertible as much as I did and we'd ride with the top down all the time unless it was too cold.

"It may not be practical," she said one time when a rain storm caught us with the top down, "but us girls got to have some frivolities. Right?" I agreed. We struggled but couldn't get it to pop up. Soaking wet, we laughed all the way to the nearest garage, then shivered inside while the mechanic worked on it.

But that hot day in August, 1977, we were plenty warm as we crossed over the river and turned south on Highway 49 down through Mississippi, heading for the Gulf Coast. I could see by the map we would have made better time if we'd hit the Interstate, but Mama didn't like to drive the Interstate. "There's nothing to see," she'd say, "and no place to stop to eat or anything."

What she meant was there were no country bars and honky tonks on the Interstate. We traveled a lot and stopped whenever Mama wanted. I saw the inside of plenty of those dim smoky places but it was okay with me. As long as I was with Mama. The bartender would fix me a big Coke and some popcorn and talk to me while Mama flirted. I'd watch her and the other grownups with their cigarettes and hold my straw like it was a cigarette. Oh, she'd stop for me too, if I saw a Dairy Queen or needed to use the bathroom. We'd spend the night in a motel and sometimes—I never knew when it was coming—Mama would announce at breakfast in a café we'd never seen before, "Well, Sister Sue, I kind of like this town. Think I'll get me a job today and we'll stay here for awhile."

She never had trouble getting a job, being a good waitress and beautiful too. Anywhere we stayed more than a week or two, she'd send me to school. By the time I graduated from high school, my list of schools totaled twenty-seven.

The traffic was light that day as we burned up the highway. The wind blew our hair and the sun scorched our faces. We had music on the radio, but when the radio blasted nothing but static we sang "99 Bottles of Beer" and "Jesus Loves Me" and every song we knew—all with equal enthusiasm. She seemed more like a sister than a mother most of the time, laughing at the words we'd miss. Back then, she didn't seem serious like other adults. Wherever we went, we had fun.

We stopped around noon and got sandwiches and Cokes at a drive-in burger place. She studied the Mississippi road map while we ate, then spread it out on the table, shoving our paper plates and plastic forks aside. She stabbed at the map with one long red fingernail. "Here's where we'll spend the night—Yazoo City. Doesn't that sound like a fun place to stay, Susie Q? Yazoo City."

"Yazoo City," I repeated. I liked the sound of Yazoo but it seemed like a funny name for a city.

We drove on into the afternoon. The sun was still high and the wind kept a warm breeze blowing across my face. We made up a silly song about Yazoo City and sang it all afternoon. We never wrote the words down and all I remember is "there's a big adventure in Yazoo City, and to miss it would be a gosh-darn pity."

Dinkins Motel was typical of other places we stayed—a building in the front close to the road with a big orange lighted "Office" sign on top and "Vacancy" below. You could see a swimming pool behind it and then a long row of doors. I tried to guess which door would be ours. Right next to the office a larger building was labeled "Cafe and Lounge" and had a "Pabst Blue Ribbon" sign in the window.

"You can swim if you want to." Mama stopped in front of the office and got out of the car. "Back in a minute."

Ten minutes later, she was unlocking the door to number eleven. "It overlooks the pool," she said. "Perfect."

The pool was alive with noisy people—kids and parents—all having a good time. I couldn't wait to get in the water. "Let's go swimming, Mama."

"Oh, honey, you go if you want to. I'm ready for a shower and a beer."

I was disappointed but I didn't want to go without her. "I'll just stay with you," I said.

One of the men in the pool let out a wolf whistle that could be heard even above the noise of splashing kids. Mama had dressed up in a short red skirt, high heel red shoes and a white blouse with ruffles. Her hair fell over her shoulders. I put on clean shorts and a t-shirt and brushed my brown hair back off my face. There was no doubt about who the guy was whistling at. Mama smiled and put a little more sway in her walk toward the restaurant.

"Let it Be" was playing on the jukebox that lit up the back wall in the lounge. We sat at the booth closest to it so we could hear the music real good. A short-haired waitress with her mouth full of chewing gum brought menus and asked, "What y'all want to drink?"

"She'll have a Coke and I'll have a Miller Lite." Mama smiled and added, "I got to keep my figger."

"Well, honey, I noticed when you came in that you got one worth keeping," the waitress said.

"Well, thank you very much," Mama said. She loved getting compliments.

We drank our drinks and ate our meal listening to one Beatles song after another. Mama said she was tired and she didn't talk much. We watched couples come and go and men gather at the bar. She got another beer and I got ice cream. "Our dessert," she said.

A big man with a long pony tail walked from behind the bar over to our booth. "You want some more Coke, little lady?"

"Okay," I said and held out my empty glass to him.

I finished my ice cream and yawned.

"You're a sleepy little girl, aren't you?" Mama swigged her beer and took a puff on her cigarette. "You better get to bed."

I was sleepy and it was no fun just sitting in that booth. She dug into her purse and got the room key.

"You go on, sweetie, get yourself in bed and I'll be along in a little." She handed me the key. "Come give Mama a kiss."

I kissed her and left with her reminding me to lock myself in and go to bed.

Banging on the door woke me up when it was still dark. I turned on the light and realized Mama wasn't in the bed. "Who's there?" I asked at the door.

"It's me," she whispered. "Let me in."

I turned the knob and she burst into the dingy room looking like a glamour queen. "Have I got news for you, Su Su! Just you wait."

"What time is it?"

"Oh, I don't know." She looked at her watch. "Five o'clock, I guess. I didn't know it was so late. But sweetheart, I've met the man."

I crawled back in bed and closed my eyes. I'd heard that before and I didn't care. It wasn't worth staying awake for.

When I next opened my eyes she was sitting cross-legged on the bed beside me singing "Are You Lonesome Tonight," layering polish over polish on her fingernails and smoking a cigarette. She couldn't wait to tell me all about it. "You're not gonna believe who I danced with all night, Susie Q." She grabbed my shoulder and shook me awake. "None other than the famous Elvis Presley—my idol."

That brought me to attention. "Elvis Presley!" Wow, I

thought, a movie star, rock star and world famous person. What was he doing here in this ordinary motel in Yazoo City? "Are you sure, Mama? Was it really Elvis?"

She laughed and hugged me when I scooted up beside her on the bed. "No doubt about it, sugar, it was the real Elvis." She screwed the top on her polish and blew on her fingernails. "He'll be back tonight."

"Well, tell me everything," I said. "Is he handsome? Did he have on his white suit with sequins on it? Did he sing to you?"

"Yes, yes, yes, and he held me close and told me I was the best dancer he'd ever met."

"But why is he here, Mama?" I asked. I'd never seen a movie star any place else we'd ever been. I assumed they all lived in Hollywood or New York City or Paris. "He must be a millionaire or a billionaire."

"I'm sure he's very rich, but well—he's from here, I mean Mississippi. And you know, his home is in Memphis." She had hopped off the bed and picked up the hairbrush. "Get dressed, baby, and let's go eat breakfast."

"Uh, are we staying here?"

She cut her eyes around and looked at me like I had lost my mind. "What do you think? Course we are."

In the restaurant, she walked to the same booth where we had eaten the night before. She touched the dingy plastic seat lightly, as if it was almost too precious to sit on. "This is where we sat," she said, smiling. "Together—on the same side."

"I thought y'all danced together."

"Sweetie, you don't understand. You can't dance every minute—not when you're together almost the whole night. We sat here and had some drinks—and cuddled."

Cuddled? Mama looked dreamy-eyed for sure. Kind of

like people in the movies after they've been kissing a lot.

A different waitress—this one was fat and plain—brought a coffee pot over and poured Mama a cup without even asking. Then she turned to me. "What can I get you to drink?" She smiled a half smile and showed her jack-o-lantern mouth. I got tickled thinking about her with a candle lighting up between her teeth.

"Su Su," Mama said, patting my hand. "Tell her what you want and stop acting silly."

"A chocolate milkshake," I said, "and a jelly donut."

Mama laughed out loud. "Jelly donut—that's what he eats," she said. "How did you come up with that?" Before I could answer, she told the waitress to bring her some toast and orange juice.

I shrugged my shoulders. "Mama, what about Priscilla? Is she here too?"

"Honey, they've been divorced for years. Elvis is free as a bird. And I'm here to tell you—he's crazy about me." She sipped her coffee, blinking her eyes. I noticed how long her eyelashes were. She looked more beautiful than ever.

"Is Elvis gonna have breakfast here?" I asked, my mouth full of jelly donut.

"Not hardly," she said. "Wipe the chocolate off your face, Suzie. Rock stars always sleep late. They don't eat breakfast 'til two or three in the afternoon. But he'll probably be out by the pool later on."

Wonderful! I was going to get to swim.

I did, too. We spent most of the day at the pool—me in the water, Mama stretched out on a chaise lounge rubbing sun screen on her everywhere the bikini didn't cover. Waiting for Elvis, that's what we did.

About four o'clock the bartender came out to the pool and sat down beside Mama. They were talking and I didn't hear what was said until Mama screamed.

"Oh, no, I don't believe it," Mama screamed. "It's a lie. He was here last night."

I stopped splashing in the water to listen.

"It's true," the burly man said. "Been on the news all day. He died in Memphis at the Baptist Hospital. Had a heart attack, according to Dr. Nichopoulos. But some people think it was drugs."

"It's not true," Mama said. She was sobbing. I climbed out of the pool and went to her side. She didn't even notice that I splashed water on her. "We danced all night." She reached out and grabbed his arm just above his wrist. "You saw us together. You know it's true."

"I wasn't paying attention to who you danced with, ma'am. I was busy mixing drinks."

I put my wet arms around her shoulder and hugged her. She was shaking. I didn't have a clue what to say.

"I won't believe it 'til I see it in the paper," she said. "Even if I do I still won't believe it. Elvis was here last night—all night. I danced with him. They've got the wrong man in that hospital in Memphis and nobody can convince me otherwise."

We stayed in Yazoo City for a week waiting for Elvis to come back, all the time hearing on the radio about his death. Mama read every word that was written in the newspaper. We watched the funeral on TV. Thousands of people stood in line at Graceland, trying to get in.

Mama began to talk to herself—or Elvis maybe. She said a lot of things about her future with Elvis, always starting with, "Me and Elvis ..."

She was convinced he'd be back for her as soon as he escaped the clutches of the Memphis doctors or Hollywood big shots—whoever it was who'd hatched up a plot to keep them apart. I asked her one time why so many people came to his funeral if he wasn't even dead.

"Oh, they had a body all right," she said. "Probably somebody dressed up to look like him. You can fool lots of folks but you can't fool Lula Thompson. No, ma'am. I know who I danced with, who held me in his arms. I know who told me he'd be back for me. It was Elvis!"

We never did get to the Gulf Coast that summer. Mama got a job waiting tables at the café at Dinkins and we stayed in Yazoo City for a few weeks. I swam every day with the manager's three kids. The oldest one, Henry, taught me to dive off the board without holding my nose. When she wasn't working, Mama sat in the sun beside the pool smoking and drinking Cokes.

By the end of summer, she had given up on Elvis coming back and in fact had a new theory. It was this: if he was actually dead, somehow on his way to the next life, he had made his way to Yazoo City and danced with her all night. He would wait for her there in the next life where she would one day join him. She felt a kinship with him that nobody could destroy—even when they told her she was crazy. And a lot of people said just that. Crazy, nuts, hallucinating, fool were some of the words they used to describe her.

We moved to Memphis and rented a room in a boarding house close to Sun Records. Mama got a job at The Waffle Shop and I started to Bellevue School. Her letter writing began after we found that portable typewriter in the Midtown Pawn Shop.

There were lots of Elvis sightings in the years to come and every one of them set Mama off again. "Maybe I was right all along," she'd say. "Maybe he is still alive. He could've been hurt or sick and couldn't get back to me. He might still be looking for me."

When the sighting wasn't too far away, Mama would take a few days off work, take me out of school and off we'd go looking for Elvis. Once we went all the way to Clinton, Oklahoma. As we drove into town, we spotted the Oklahoma Route 66 Museum. A gleaming pink Cadillac filled the front showcase window and across the street, a motel marquee with big bold letters declared: ELVIS SLEPT HERE. We had come to the right place. We stayed there four days waiting for him to turn up. It turned out one of the maids had seen him when she went in to clean a room. Mama found the maid and questioned her about her experience.

"She didn't really see Elvis," Mama said as we headed out of town toward Memphis. "This was a wasted trip."

Aren't they all? I wanted to say, but didn't. We settled into a routine and stayed in Memphis for two years before Mama got the wanderlust again. We drove to the Gulf Coast and Mama stopped talking about Elvis. We stopped chasing after sightings but still made the pilgrimage to Memphis every year to celebrate his birth. She wouldn't go for his death because "that would be admitting it's true. And we're not really sure."

So that's it. She spent the rest of her life trying to sell her story. Was it the hope of making a lot of money? That was part of it. She thought her ship had almost come in but not quite and she had to help bring it to shore. She also believed it with all her heart. I did too, because you have to believe in your mama. Now I don't know. Maybe it was true and maybe it was only a dream. But one thing is certain. She never had any doubt about it. Elvis lived in her heart every day of her life.

In a way, they were kindred spirits—both of them done in by their bad habits. And who knows? Maybe they're dancing together now in the next life.

More Precious Than Rubies

By Beverly Williams

I hand over the last child to his mother and begin straightening the Sunday School room. A roomful of four-year-olds is hard to manage. My own are away at college now, and I don't regret it. The empty nest is peaceful.

"I don't know how you do it, Rachel," says the young mother, fashionable in her short-skirted suit. "You are the perfect minister's wife."

I just smile. I teach this Sunday School class of little hellions because volunteers are scarce. When there's a job that no one else will take, the minister's wife fills in the gaps. I keep telling myself I'm going to refuse to do it any longer. Then Carl tells me how he couldn't get along without me and quotes some scripture about a good woman being more precious than rubies. I give in every time.

"You're an angel, Rachel," he says. Weak is what I am.

I put away the crayons and paper. There is dirt in the corners of the room and dust on the window sills. The vestry fired the sexton last week after they found out he'd been pilfering the communion wine. If the poor man is hard up enough to drink that cheap stuff, I say let him have it. One tiny sip is enough for me.

I close the door and head to the bathroom. It could stand to be cleaned, too, but I am not, repeat not, going to do it. I glance at my watch, then go up the steps from the Sunday School rooms to the church.

St. Bartholomew's Episcopal Church is as familiar to me as my house, but it gives me little comfort. My faith has been tested and instead of triumphing over my doubts, it remains frayed and tattered. I still believe in God, but it seems as if He no longer believes in me.

I slip through the side door and into my customary pew. Right side of the church, sixth row. I'd rather sit further back, but Carl says the minister's wife should sit close to the front. I pull down the kneeler to say my private prayers, but I have a hard time concentrating, so I just ask God to watch over the children away at school. Keep Jeffrey from drinking too much, and don't let Stephanie get pregnant. Amen.

I sit back and mouth a hello to the Everharts across the aisle, and lean over to pat Susan Lewis on the shoulder. She lost her husband last month after a long bout with cancer. Only thirty-nine. You can tell she's still reeling. People nearby smile at me and I smile back, thinking of all the times I have smiled when there was no happiness inside me.

The organ music swells and the congregation stands as the processional begins. It looks as if the crowd is going to be small today, which always makes Carl unhappy. He takes it personally. It's cold and rainy, the kind of day when people find an excuse to skip church and stay home by the fire. I'd do it myself, but I can only get away with it about once a year.

The acolyte comes in first, carrying the cross. I bow my head as it passes. Then the choir, then the young assistant rector, then Carl. He's carrying a hymnal, his reading glasses perched on the end of his nose, his voice soaring with holy fervor. He looks so spiritual, some might think it's an act, but it's not. When he's in church, it's like the Holy Spirit enters his body, and he's transformed.

The first time I saw him, we were in college. It was spring, a really warm day, and everyone was outside, wearing shorts, cutting classes, lying on blankets on the ground. He was playing frisbee with some other guys when the frisbee sailed off course, over to where I was sitting on the ground, trying to study. He came sprinting over to catch it, running across my blanket, almost crashing into me.

"Hey!" I yelled. "Watch out."

"Hey yourself," he said, flashing me a brilliant smile. With his long hair and blue eyes, he looked like a Hollywood Jesus.

A few minutes later, he abandoned the other Frisbee players and plopped himself on my blanket. Uninvited but not unwelcome. And that was the end of my semi-engagement to a pre-law student and my plans to be a magazine editor.

As he passes me, he gives me that special intimate look that seems like a combination of a blessing and a sexual invitation. It never fails to bring a physical response—I feel it now. Of course, after all these years, there are times when he seems as ordinary as any other man. Things dull down in marriage. The flash and dazzle of sex becomes routine, the sharpness of it fades. Still, there are times …

My eyes are on Carl as he moves down the aisle. Then I notice her. On the left side, second row. I know her. A young divorcee, new to the congregation. Leslie something, I can't remember her last name. Pretty, but no taste, the kind of woman you want to take in hand and show her how to fix herself up. Carl looks her way. I can't see his face, but I can see hers. The eager, starstruck look. My heart sinks.

But perhaps I'm mistaken. I've become so suspicious. Many women idolize clergymen, even the average-looking ones. Carl is movie star handsome, which is dangerous enough, but it's more than that. He has a quality of empathy that makes each person feel unique. Chosen. Even men. Particularly women.

It's been two years since the last one. We were in Memphis then, at a fashionable but conservative church. I knew something was going on; Carl denied it, but the signs were there. She was his secretary. Married also. They thought they were being discreet, but there was no way they could hide it. It careened off them like atomic energy, filling the room with wildly zig-zagging protons and neutrons. The gossip spread like wildfire through the congregation, and I could feel the curious, pitying eyes on me. The vestry met and confronted Carl. He stonewalled, as if he thought they wouldn't dare contradict him. Eventually the bishop got into the mix, and Carl confessed. There was tearful contrition and much praying. Promises to never stray again. The bishop banished Carl to Mississippi, to a small town church desperate for a rector.

I was devastated. And frightened by my anger. Still, I thought if he got away from her, we could make it together. But no matter how hard I tried and how much I prayed, I couldn't forgive him. I almost gave up and left, but he pleaded with me to stay. He promised never to see her again, though I suspected there were phone calls. He swore she meant nothing to him, that it was just the devil tempting him, but I think he was really in love with her. He couldn't hide the misery in his eyes. In the end, I stayed. I said it was for the children. The truth is that I felt I would die without him.

And I've been fairly happy here, as happy as I could be with my marriage in shambles.

Lately he's seemed more content. And with the children gone, we have sex more often. I've been thinking that it's finally going to be over, that I will at last be able to forgive.

Carl reaches the front of the church and turns to face the congregation. His eyes flick to the second row, meet hers momentarily. I can see them both. Oh, God, there's no mistaking it. I'm sure now. I feel as if I'm about to fly into a million pieces. It's not over; it's just beginning. It will never, ever be over.

I push my way out of the pew and stumble from the church. People stare at me. I vaguely hear someone ask if I'm all right. I don't look at Carl, but I can imagine his surprise, maybe even alarm. This is not like me. I am so predictable, so stable. Good old Rachel. The rock of Gibraltar.

I walk through the rain to our house next door to the church. It belongs to them, not to us. We don't even lock the doors in this peaceful little Mississippi town. I'm calm now. I go into Carl's study and find what I am looking for.

I slip back into the church and sit in an empty pew alone in the back. Carl is sitting in the throne-like chair at the front while the assistant rector reads the New Testament lesson. He smiles at me, looking relieved. I kneel and pray for courage, pray for my children.

Then I slip my hand inside my purse. I wrap my hand around the cold steel. It warms under my fingers, gives me comfort. It is going to be over now. At last.

Auction Fever

By Nina Salley Hepburn

The birds-eye maple Welsh dresser was the very first inanimate object that I actually fell in love with. I spotted it during the one-hour preview period before the auction started and my heart literally skipped a beat. I reached out and touched it—carefully as if it might give under the pressure of my hand—and felt a shudder flit through my body. No doubt about it. My name was on it. I had to have it! When I showed it to Fred, he resisted momentarily.

"Aw, Mabel, that thing must be seven feet tall. Where on earth would we put it if we had it? Too big for the dining room."

"Yes, but just *feel* it," I said. "And Fred, think of the display space. It will hold our entire collection of Hummel figurines, perhaps some of the Carnival glass, too."

He stroked the smooth golden patina of the top. Years of use and polishing had worn the wood to a satiny feel. I didn't have to say a word—just waited for the piece itself to win him over.

Not that we needed it. Not that we could really afford it.

Not that we had an empty spot in our house that cried out for such a large piece of furniture. But it was one of a kind! We began discussing which wall of the dining room it would best fit, which chair or cupboard or server would have to go to make room for it.

The other problem was that we had only planned to spend two hundred dollars total for whatever purchases we made that Sunday afternoon and already we had spied a few other treasures we lusted after. Still it didn't occur to either of us that we wouldn't get the Welsh dresser. *It was meant to be ours.*

Before viewing the day's offerings, we had signed in and picked up our bidding card—number seventeen.

We started going to auctions soon after I had a miscarriage and the doctor said I couldn't have more children. I was desperate for something to do, so when I saw the ad in the paper about an auction, I asked Fred to go. We bought a magnificent flow-blue pitcher that now holds silk daisies and graces one end of the faux fireplace mantle in our cozy den. No one would ever notice the teensy little chip on the lip of the pitcher. I keep that side turned toward the wall. We decided then and there that seventeen would be our number.

Of course, the auctioneer never brings out the good stuff early in the auction. If he did, people would grab it, spend all their money, and leave. Then who would buy the junk? Nobody. But we don't mind waiting. We have the time. The good stuff usually starts to trickle out about four or five o'clock. And we do try not to purchase anything strictly on impulse. Instead, we bide our time.

Good things come to those who wait. I remind Fred of that.

Sometimes Fred will slip up though. When the spotter

comes at him holding a genuine sterling silver candy dish or an early 1900's flat iron, begging for a raise on the bid—just one dollar more—well, Fred can't seem to say no. I poke him with the blunt end of my pen, but he gets so carried away, he'll nod and first thing we know, the floor all around our chairs is covered up with mostly worthless trinkets.

"Now, Fred," I reminded him that Sunday, "remember what we're here to buy. Don't let them hook you on a bunch of useless junk."

"Don't you be worrying about me, Mabel," he said.

He stuffed the last big bite of a mustard-smothered corn dog into his mouth and washed it down with a gulp of iced tea. They sell food at the auctions and we usually eat lunch at our seats. It's cheaper and faster too, than stopping at McDonald's or Wendy's on the way. Besides, it's fun—kind of like eating at the circus.

"Who was it that bought that nineteenth century curling iron that you'd have to heat in the fire if you wanted to use it. And I guess you noticed we don't have anything in the house to burn a fire in. And what about that high top shoe buttoner? I haven't noticed you wearing any buttoned up shoes lately."

"I think I'll get me another cup of coffee before the bidding starts," I said, ignoring his jab at me.

He laughed so hard he almost choked on the last of his iced tea.

"Got your goat, didn't I?" he said. "You know what I said is true. And get me another iced tea and a Baby Ruth candy bar."

Well, yes, it was true. I did weaken a time or two. But I had vowed to turn over a new leaf and only buy things we really needed—or at least really wanted.

While I was in line for the coffee, I noticed Emma Lou

Rogers. Oh, dear, I thought. Trouble, with a capital T. She and her husband, Al are known as the "last of the big spenders" when it comes to auctions. The story is that they inherited a fortune from her spinster aunt in Texas whose property just bubbled with oil. If those two get their eye on something, you may as well forget it. They will bid against you just for the meanness of it. And nine times out of ten, they'll take it home. The only satisfaction is that you made them pay way more than the thing was worth.

"Why, hello, Mabel," she said—a condescending tone in her syrupy sweet voice. She waved her left hand in front of my face. "I noticed you and Fred got your lucky number. Anything special you got your eye on today?"

"Oh, nothing in particular," I said nonchalantly. I tried to avoid looking at the huge diamonds on her fingers, but it appeared there was a new flasher since the last time I saw her. She looked a little heavier too. I took some satisfaction in the fact that her figure had increased in proportion to the size of her jewels. "We just came today 'cause it's a rainy day and there was nothing else to do."

I wasn't about to give her the satisfaction of knowing I wanted that dresser. Maybe some miracle would happen and she'd spend her money before it came up. Or maybe she didn't have room for my Welsh dresser. That was doubtful, though, since she and Al had built a great big gaudy mansion right on the main road coming into town. The house has about a dozen columns two stories tall stuck out front for everyone to see. And a big stone mailbox at the edge of the driveway with their names on it in huge print.

"Guess lots of folks are here for entertainment," she said as she glanced around the room. "But there is quite a crowd today. No doubt lots of serious buyers. Probably won't be any bargains." She had reached the counter. "I'll have a hamburger, two hot dogs, two orders of fries and two diet cokes.

"Yeah, everybody better be prepared to *pay* for what they get," she continued. "No steals this afternoon."

She just had to rub it in. She might as well have told me she was going to buy that dresser right out from under me. I got my coffee, Fred's tea and candy, and rushed back to my seat.

"Fred, we can't spend a penny on anything. Not a penny. I've got to have that Welsh dresser and those Rogers people are here. She as much as told me she was buying it. So just sit on your hand when the bidding starts."

"Well, you better sit on yours too."

I sipped my black coffee, willing myself not to glance at the prized dresser even for a second, and settled back to wait. The room filled with people, crowding in all around us and even lining the walls on both sides of the smoky room.

Harlan Smally had the typical auctioneer's voice—raspy from years of overuse. Too bad people aren't more like fine furniture, I thought. Lasting forever and improving with age and use instead of deteriorating. The spotters began bringing out small collectables as Harlan started his spiel.

"Here's a pretty little cup and saucer—got Bavarian on the bottom. Who'll give me five dollars for it?" He handed it to the skinny spotter with a bad cough. He in turn brought it out close to the crowd, trying to tempt everyone to go for it as Harlan continued ...

"Five dollar, five dollar, who'll gi' me five dollar? Okay, then, who'll gi' me four? Four, four, four. Where? I got three from the back. Three dollar, got three, who gi' me four? Got it. Who gi' me five? Worth it. Got four, four, four, gi' me five, five, who'll gi' me five? Four, four, four, is that all?" He slammed the gavel on the table. "Sold—four dollars."

That's the way the afternoon went. I kept an eye on Fred, making sure he didn't let those guys tempt him to bid. We *had* to wait for the Welsh dresser.

Finally they brought it out to the stage. It was so heavy three men had to move it. I held my breath. Harlan described the bird's eye grain of the wood and emphasized the hand turned spindles that accented the ledges, then started the bidding at one hundred dollars.

The bidding went fast and furious, passing our top price. Emma Lou Rogers jumped in at four hundred fifty dollars. I had known she would. I waited. The bidding slowed.

"Got four fifty—who'll gi' me five? Five, five, five, five hundred. Where's five?"

She's not getting my Welsh dresser for four hundred and fifty dollars, I thought. I grabbed the card from Fred and held it up.

The spotter was on me immediately. "Got five hundred." Then it was right on to asking for five fifty. I watched Emma Lou. The spotter had turned to her. She showed her card. Then he was back to me. I hesitated but caved in. I had it at six hundred. Emma Lou jumped all the way to seven. She was closing me out!

That'll be the day, I thought. The contest was between the two of us. I could bid seven fifty. But maybe—just maybe—she had set a limit. I decided to beat her at her game, so I jumped to one thousand dollars—five times what we had planned to spend!

Harlan jumped to fifteen hundred and the spotter moved over to Emma Lou. I waited. Emma Lou was silent. Harlan dropped back to eleven hundred, almost pleading. I thought she'd go for it. I wouldn't bid again, I decided, no matter what.

Then I heard the gavel. "Sold—one thousand dollars—to

number seventeen."

"Fred, we got it," I said. I could hardly believe it. I felt like I'd given birth. It was the child I always wanted and never had.

The Welsh dresser is even more beautiful today than it was the day we bought it. It occupies the longest wall in the dining room and everyone who enters the house admires it. Although I have to admit the numerous odd pieces of china, pottery and bric a brac scattered about—a temporary situation—do not enhance its beauty. The red milk paint cabinet on the same wall is also a distraction, but we will find a better place for it eventually. Looking back, it seems we bought the dresser for a song. Best of all, we out-bid Emma Lou Rogers. And it's worth far more today than we paid.

Five years ago—the year Fred retired from the Post Office—I decided we needed to unload some of the excess we have collected during years of auctioneering. Fred resisted. He gets attached to things. In fact, if something spends one night in this house, as far as he's concerned it's like a member of the family.

"We'll have a garage sale," I said one morning after breakfast. "I put an ad in the newspaper for next Saturday, so we've got our work cut out for us."

"I hate garage sales," Fred said. "You get all kinds of people snooping through your stuff. They could be crooks—come back at night to steal you blind. We have plenty of room in the attic—anything you're tired of, just tell me and I'll take it up there. Or we could take it to the garage. It's nice and dry there. Won't hurt a thing."

"Now that you mention it, I'd like to park the car in the garage. If we sold some of the tools you never use and some of the excess furniture we don't need. Remember that old beat-up roll top desk you bought last year? You were planning to refinish it. It's still out there taking up space, covered with dust. What about that rocking chair that needs a new cane bottom? Remember when you bought that? You never did learn to repair the cane. A garage sale will solve all our problems."

"Mabel, I don't want to talk about it. I'll get around to fixing all those things now that I'm retired. We don't have anything we can't use. Let's drop the subject."

"Fred, you've been retired six whole months and you haven't fixed anything yet. We need to have a sale."

I spent the entire day going through closets and drawers. Some of our wonderful treasures gleaned from years at auctions were hidden—many in the same boxes we'd brought them home in. Depression glass in pinks and greens. Plates, sugar bowls, creamers, platters—every conceivable item one could imagine. They were indeed priceless collectables. And to think merchants had once given them away to customers.

I found lovely oil lamps from the days before electricity. Most of them had never been wired and the tarnished brass ones still waited to be polished. We didn't need any more light in the house, but these beautiful testaments to the ingenuity of the past would certainly enhance a bedroom chest or dining room buffet. They could be electrified and used to replace some of the rather ordinary lamps we used.

After hours of sorting through the results of years of collecting, I had three definite garage sale items put aside: a badly stained white linen tablecloth that was too small for our table, a turn-of-the-century cookbook printed in German, and a large metal milk can painted bright yellow. These were only a few of the purchases Fred had been suckered into. I distinctly remembered each one and how I had scolded.

"I hope you're satisfied," Fred said at lunch. We were in the den, our food on folding tray tables. "You've got so much stuff on the table we don't even have a place to eat."

"My point, Fred. And I could use a little help getting ready for the sale."

"I hate garage sales! I won't be a party to it. If you want to sell some of *your* things, let's take 'em to the auction. But I don't want to sell anything of mine. The subject is closed."

I cancelled my newspaper ad and instead Fred loaded up a few things we decided we could part with. The half a truckload didn't make much of a dent, but it was a start, I told myself.

"Now that we're taking all my good stuff to the auction, let's not even think about buying anything else," Fred said on the way to deliver our treasures. "That way, we won't have to go through all this again."

"You're right." But I was thinking we would do this very thing again—and soon. "We don't even have to come back tomorrow for the auction."

Fred backed the truck up to the loading dock and some of the men there helped him take the stuff inside. In the meantime, I wandered around to see what else would be in the sale. Just out of curiosity. Mostly junk, I thought. Mismatched chairs, rickety tables, lamps with no shades, and the usual assortment of odd dishes—none of them interesting.

I started back toward the truck—satisfied there was absolutely nothing there that I could possibly want. Then I saw it. The most beautiful Hoosier cabinet ever made. Reminded me of the one my grandmother used in her kitchen when I was a child. The light oak finish was in perfect condition. The white enameled pullout was without a chip. I opened the large door at the top and was surprised to see the original flour bin. The sifter still worked.

I could hardly believe it. Such a fine kitchen piece, one any collector would be delighted to have. But we had no room in our small kitchen. What with the dry sink and the jelly cupboard, plus the necessary appliances, it was packed full.

Disheartened, I almost told the Hoosier goodbye. Then I remembered a wall in the sunroom that was just about the right size. There was nothing on that wall except a little plant rack. That could be moved anywhere—even outside. The auction fever rose in me. I had to have the Hoosier cabinet.

"Fred, Fred," I called as I walked toward him, trying to appear calm. There was no doubt in my mind. Fred would love it too.

⚜

Old Maid

By Beverly Williams

"It's eight-twenty. Breakfast isn't ready." My brother's voice is accusing.

"I overslept."

I didn't really. It's just that he is so prissy, the way he wants things to be at exact times, and I like to shake him up a little. Besides, he could fix his own breakfast. It's only corn flakes and bananas. Every day.

We sit down at the kitchen table ten minutes later, and Julian says the blessing. We eat our cereal in silence, except for the clink of his spoon against the side of the bowl and the way he slurps up his milk and cereal, like some bad-mannered animal. Mother taught us not to make noises when we eat. I think he does it on purpose.

"Today is laundry day," he says. "I want to get to the Laundromat early, before it's crowded."

"Can't we do it tomorrow?"

"No. We have to go today. I need clean socks."

"I hate the Laundromat. Why don't we get our washing machine fixed?"

"I told you, Sister. Next month. After our checks come in."

"Why do you always get to decide what we spend the money on? It's my money, too."

He looks at me like I'm a two-year-old, and a stupid one at that. "You wouldn't know how. Someone has to manage the money, and it's me."

We both get a check from the government, for disability. Julian got his first. He used to work at a grocery store, but he kept getting fired because he was always telling the manager how to do things. Then he started getting too nervous to go to work, and our family doctor sent him to the mental health clinic. A psychiatrist said he has obsessive-compulsive disorder and he started getting a check every month, so now he doesn't work at all.

I didn't work while Mother was alive, because she said I needed to be home to take care of the house while she was at her job, so I just did some baby-sitting for the neighbors. Then after Mother died, I guess I was depressed because I cried all the time. I missed her so, and I still do. Anyway, I went to the mental health clinic and they got me disability, too. I feel better now, but I still get a check every month.

"Go get your laundry together," says bossy Julian, looking at his watch. "We'll leave in ten minutes."

He picks up a sponge and wipes the kitchen counters, even though I have already done it and there's not a speck on them.

I stuff my dirty clothes in two pillowcases. There was something I planned to do this morning, but I will do it this afternoon. When Julian takes his nap.

Julian always takes a nap after lunch, like an old man. He's only forty two, but he's old in his head. Always has been.

I change into my second-best slacks and a shirt I ironed last night, then leave Julian a note telling him I have gone to the drug store. I slip out the back door and walk six blocks to McRae's Nursery. By the time I get there, I'm sweaty. I wish I had taken the bus, but it's too late now. I hope I don't smell.

I take the newspaper clipping out of my purse and look at it one more time, even though I have it memorized. *Nursery help wanted: Care for plants, assist with customers, experience preferred. Apply in person.*

I take a deep breath and go inside. The woman behind the counter is talking to a customer.

"Your clematis likes sun, but you've got to keep its feet wet. You'll need to mulch."

I wait, my palms getting sweaty, until she looks up.

"Can I help you?"

I want to run out the door, but my feet won't move. "I'm here about the job," I squeak. "In the newspaper."

"Walter," she yells, "someone here about the job."

An old couple over by the garden tools look around at me. I feel like crawling into a watering can, like Peter Rabbit. Instead, I pretend to examine a rack of flower seeds. I've never liked to be noticed.

A man comes out from somewhere in the back. The woman behind the counter nods in my direction. I can see him giving me an appraising look. He's probably deciding I won't do. Or maybe the job is already filled.

"You're here about the job?" he asks.

"Yes, sir."

"Come on back to the office."

I follow him down a short hall to a cluttered office and sit in the wooden chair he indicates. I'm glad to sit down, since my knees feel like they might give way any minute. He gives me an application to fill out. When I hand it back to him, he glances at it to read my name. I see the nameplate on his desk. Walter McRae. It's wooden, the name etched in, little pieces of dust permanently shellacked onto it. It looks like something his son made at summer camp.

"So, Alice," he says, "have you ever worked in a nursery before?"

"No, sir."

"What other work experience have you had?" Now he looks at my application.

"I've done a lot of babysitting," I say, "and I work in my garden." Which is not entirely true. Since Mother died, I've let the garden go, but I've been thinking lately that I might try to get the beds back in shape.

"Well," he says, "we actually need a person with some work experience. Lots of customer contact." His voice is regretful, like he's giving someone bad news.

I should have known it was a mistake to come here. A thirty-eight-year-old woman with no work experience whatsoever? He must think I'm crazy. Maybe I am. The neighborhood kids think so. A weird, looney tunes old maid who lives with her even loonier brother. Old maid Alice, that's me. Tears of self-pity well up in my eyes and spill over to my cheeks. I duck my head so Mr. McRae won't notice. But he does. He looks alarmed.

"I could use somebody in the back," he says. "Watering and moving the plants around. Are you strong?"

Hope surges through me, making me brave. "Oh, yes, sir. Very strong."

"Last person I had working back there claimed he hurt his back. I need somebody strong. Don't want another workman's comp claim."

"Oh, no sir, I wouldn't do anything like that." I'm not sure what a workman's comp claim is, but I'll agree to anything.

"Job pays minimum wage," he says.

I nod. Does this mean he's going to hire me?

"Can you start tomorrow?"

"Yes, sir. Thank you." The tears threaten again, but this time it's gratitude. I blink them back. I don't want him to think I'm a crybaby.

"Eight o'clock." He stands up, and I figure I'm dismissed. I want to know more, like what I should wear and how often I get paid, but I scurry away before he can change his mind.

When I get home, Julian is watching "Jeopardy," yelling out the answers, even though nobody else is there.

"Where have you been?" he says, when a commercial comes on. His voice is stern, like he's my father, instead of just my brother.

"I left you a note."

"It's been two hours. You couldn't have been at the drug store that long."

"I wasn't at the drug store." I smile mysteriously. I absolutely love to bug Julian.

"Well, where were you?"

"Oh, I just had a little business to take care of."

"What kind of business could *you* have?" He can be so mean, sometimes I hate him. But he can't make me feel bad today.

"I was out getting ..." I pause dramatically "... a job."

"I don't believe you." He turns back to the TV, as Alex Trebek comes back on. I don't like Jeopardy, but I love Alex. He is one of my favorite fantasy people.

"Well, it's the truth, Mr. Smarty. I have a job at McRae's

Nursery, starting tomorrow. You'll have to fix your own breakfast. I have to be at work at eight." It feels important, saying that I have to be at work.

Julian looks at me now, his face getting red and splotchy. "You dummy! You can't get a job. We'll lose the check."

"What?"

"Your disability check, stupid. They're not going to send you money if you're working. We need that check. You have to call up McRae's and tell them you can't take the job."

I hadn't thought about the disability, but I am sure Julian is right. It makes sense. Still, I don't care. I want a job of my own.

"Why? I'll be getting money from my job."

"Minimum wage?"

"Yes, but …"

"And then you'll get fired after a couple of weeks, and where will we be? You just tell me that."

"I won't get fired." He is trying to make me cry, the way he always does, but I am not going to let him. "And I'm not quitting."

Julian sulks all evening. It's meat loaf night, which I think will get him in a better mood, but he won't even speak to me. So instead of watching television with him after supper, I go to my room. It feels so lonely when he won't talk to me, I'd rather be by myself.

I paint my toenails, just for something to do. Then I lay out my clothes for tomorrow, like Mother used to do for me when I was in school. I go in Mother's room and get her alarm clock and set it for six-thirty. I wonder if I'll be able to sleep at all, I'm so excited and nervous. A real job! I can't believe I did it. All by myself, I went out and found a job. If I had known it would feel this good, I would have done it a long time ago.

I wish I could tell Mother. Maybe I can. I close my eyes. *Guess what, Mother. I have a job. Not babysitting, either. It's a real job, at McRae's Nursery. I start tomorrow. I put out my clothes to wear tomorrow—my khaki pants and that blue plaid shirt you gave me for my birthday. Do you think that will be okay?*

I think I can imagine Mother saying she's proud of me, but that's probably just me. I open my eyes. She would probably be like Julian, worrying about everything, thinking it will never work. She even used to worry when I would babysit, like I was going to drop a baby or let a kid get run over by a car.

I want to call my friend Linda, but the phone is in the kitchen, and grouchy old Julian would hear me and that would make me self-conscious. When I get paid, I think I will get a phone for my room, so I can have telephone conversations in private, without him eavesdropping all the time. Not that I have that many conversations. Linda is about the only friend I have. And she has a boyfriend now, even though she is very fat, so we don't talk as much as we used to. When we do, it's just her talking about Dave. Girls change when they get a boyfriend.

I make a list of things I will buy with my money. Julian always takes the check I get from the government and puts it in the bank. He says it pays for all our living expenses. But I wonder. The house is paid for and we don't have a car. We never buy new clothes, except for shoes, which we get at Pay-Less. Sometimes we go to the Salvation Army used clothing store, but mostly we just wear what we have. And we never, ever eat out. Julian gives me a little money to buy my female things at the drug store. It embarrasses him if I get maxi-pads when we go to Kroger.

I know he spends money on himself. I found the magazines in his room. They were between the mattress and the box springs of his bed. Lots of them. Not just Playboy, either. Much worse, with pictures of women with their legs all spread apart. It was gross. But kind of fascinating at the same time. I didn't tell him I knew about his secret, but I like knowing. It gives me some power over him.

I read my book for a while. I like historical romance novels. They're pretty sexy, but they don't have any disgusting pictures in them. You just make them up in your mind. And the hero and the heroine always fall in love. Actually, they've been in love all through the book, they just don't know it. You think they're never going to get together, but in the end they always do. I like happy endings. I wish I could have one of my own.

I don't need the alarm clock. I am awake at five. It is nice at that time of the morning, all quiet except for the birds singing and one dog barking. I open the back door and listen. A car goes down the street.

By the time I am ready to leave for work, Julian is up.

"I need money for the bus," I say.

"I gave you money the other day."

"I had to spend some of it. I don't have enough left."

"Too bad. You should have saved it."

"Julian, that is my money, too. You don't have any right to keep it."

"I'm not keeping it. I'm using it to pay the bills for both of us. Before she died, Mother told me that I should be in control of the money. She said you don't have enough sense to manage money."

"That's not true. And I don't believe she said that."

I know Mother wouldn't say that about me. Julian is not

above making up things to win an argument. But there's no way I can prove he's wrong.

"Suit yourself. But I'm not giving you any money."

"Please, Julian. If I walk, I'll be all hot and sweaty by the time I get there." I hate begging, but I don't have any choice.

"You should have thought of that before you went out and got that job." His face gets all screwed up and ugly when he says "job."

I grab my purse and my lunch and walk out the door. On the way out, I raise my hand over my head and flip him off. It makes me feel better.

Julian gives me the silent treatment all week, but I don't care. I don't want to talk to him, either. By the time Friday finally comes, he gives me money for the bus. Trying to butter me up now. It won't work, but I don't tell him that.

Working at McRae's is harder than I thought it would be. Yesterday we got a new shipment of bedding plants and I had to help unload them, then move all the old ones to the front tables, so we could sell them first. At the end of the day, my arms and back were killing me. So far I mostly do a lot of lifting, and watering. I like watering best. The plants seem so grateful. I'm learning the names of them. Most of them are labeled and also Leon, who's my boss, tells me what they are. Leon doesn't say much, but he is nice. One day I knocked over a peony and all the dirt spilled out of the pot and some of the leaves broke off. He put it all back in and said don't worry about it.

Today is payday. I think about opening a bank account, but my check is not as much as I thought it would be, since I didn't work a full week and they take out a lot for taxes and something called FICA. I had no idea. On my lunch break, I go to the bank and cash it. I love having money that

I earned myself. Julian will try to make me give most of it to him. I am going to tell him I don't get paid till next week.

We have to work on Saturday, since it's the busy season. Just before quitting time, Leon comes over to where I am watering the pots of hybrid tea roses. He just stands there, not saying anything, and I get self-conscious. He clears his throat and I look up. I think maybe I'm not doing it right, but I'm being careful not to get any water on the leaves.

"Uh ... Alice," he finally says. "I saw you getting off the bus yesterday. I thought maybe ... would you like a ride home?"

I look up. Leon's face is sort of a blotchy red. "Oh, I just take the bus to work. I always walk home. For the exercise." Of course it's really to save money.

"Okay, sure," he says. "I just thought ..." His voice trails off and he starts to edge away. I can't believe it, but he actually seems disappointed.

"But I'd love a ride home," I say. "Thanks." Mother always taught me not to hurt anybody's feelings.

Leon's car is a dusty old Plymouth, but it's clean inside. The seats have seat covers on them and there is a little plastic saint hanging from the rear view mirror. The manure-like smell of mulch is partially masked by Glade air freshener, which I recognize because that's what we use in the bathroom at home.

I tell Leon where I live, but we don't talk. I look at him sideways so he won't notice. I had been thinking of him as older than me, but he is probably about my age. I always think authority figures are older. Not that Leon seems like much of an authority figure, but he is in charge of the back of the nursery.

"Are you married?" he asks finally.

"No." I'm surprised anyone asks. I feel like I have old

maid written all over me.

"Boyfriend?"

"Not currently." Now what in the world made me say that? I've never had a boyfriend.

"Me neither. I mean, I don't have a girlfriend."

We turn into my street. "Right there," I say. "The one on the left with the green shutters." The house looks sad and shabby, with the paint peeling on the shutters. At least Julian keeps the grass mowed. It's the only real work he does.

"Well, thanks for the ride." I open the door.

"Uh … do you like to fish?"

"I don't know. I never have." Why is he asking me this?

"I always go fishing on Sunday morning. I thought you might like to go."

I think Leon is asking me for a date. I don't know what to say. I have no experience in either accepting a date or declining.

"Unless you have something else to do."

I shake my head. We used to go to church on Sunday when Mother was living, but we don't do that anymore.

"It's fun," says Leon, like he's selling something. "You would like it."

"Okay. Yeah." I don't even care if it's not fun. I just want to be able to say I had a date.

Leon smiles. He has a tooth missing, but it's pretty far back. You don't notice when he's just talking.

"I'll pick you up at seven. You have to go early when the fish are biting."

"Okay." I get out of the car and walk up the sidewalk. I'm sure old Julian is lurking behind the mini-blinds. He's worse than an old woman, the way he spies on the neighborhood.

He pounces the minute I come in the door. "Who was

that?"

"Just a guy from work."

"You stayed out there a long time. What were you doing?"

"None of your beeswax." I swear, Julian gets on my last nerve. "Talking. Anyway, you were spying on us. You could see what we were doing."

"I don't think you should be riding around with strange men."

"He's not a strange man. He's my boss. He gave me a ride home."

"You don't know about men, Sister. Once he's got you in his car, he can take you anywhere he wants to and do whatever he pleases with you. And there wouldn't be anything you could do." His face flushes with triumphant relish as he makes this last statement. "What would the neighbors think?" I don't know why he cares, he doesn't like any of them anyway. Then, "Mother would be ashamed of you." His favorite. That one usually gets to me, but no more.

"She would not. Anyway, Leon isn't like that. And I'm going out with him tomorrow. We're going fishing."

"You most certainly are not going out with him. I won't let you."

"You can't stop me."

"I'm sorry if you don't like it, but I have to protect you. Mother told me to take care of you."

"Don't be silly, Julian. We're just going fishing. It's not even a date. And it's in the daytime."

"It doesn't matter. Things can happen in the daytime." His voice is ominous. "When he comes tomorrow, we just won't let him in."

"I can't do that. I told him I would. And he's my boss. I might get fired."

"You're going to get fired sooner or later, anyway. You're not going, and that's that."

I feel the anger boiling inside me, but I grab it and hold it in before it escapes. I can see that I have to be smart about this. Julian is basically a wimp, but when he sets his mind to something, he can be stubborn as a mule. I give a disappointed sigh.

"Maybe you're right. I don't really know him very well. I'll call him up and tell him I can't go."

"Good," says Julian. "You'll thank me for this later." I want to smack that smug look off his face.

"Supper will be a little late," I say. "I want to take a shower first."

Julian's happy because he won, so he doesn't even complain. "What are we having?"

"Ham, cream style corn, and limas. Canned biscuits." Like he didn't know. We have the same thing every Saturday night. I'm getting sick of it.

I go in the bathroom and while the water's running, I open the medicine cabinet. Aha! I find what I am looking for. The pills the doctor gave Mother when the pain got so bad at the end that she couldn't sleep. I slip the bottle into the pocket of my bathrobe.

Just before I put the supper on the table, I open three of the capsules and pour the contents into Julian's iced tea. I'm sure that will do it, since just one used to make Mother sleep till eight in the morning. But Julian weighs more, of course. I pour in one more, for good measure. Then add extra sugar, in case the pills make his tea bitter. And add salt to the limas, so he'll be thirsty and drink all his tea. I'm proud of myself for thinking of that angle.

After supper, we watch television, some boring thing about Africa on the education channel. I watch him out of the corner of my eye. When he starts to yawn and nod, I try to get him to go to bed, but he won't. By eight o'clock, he's snoring on the couch. I go in my room, lay out my clothes, and read for a while.

When I get up the next morning, Julian is still on the couch. His mouth is open and he's very still. I have a moment of panic. But I stand over him and I can see his stomach move up and down.

At ten till seven, I slip out the back door and walk down to the corner. When I see Leon's car coming, I wave.

"Hey," he says.

I get in. "I just thought I'd meet you out here. My brother's still asleep and I didn't want to wake him up."

Fishing is not as much fun as I thought it would be. I keep losing my bait and Leon has to put more on. I only catch one little fish and Leon doesn't catch any. I'm probably bad luck for him. Then I start thinking about Julian and worrying what I will tell him. He's bound to be awake when I get back. I decide I will have Leon let me off a block away and then I will tell Julian I went for a walk. A long one.

When I get out of the car, I say, "Thanks for taking me fishing. I had a nice time."

"Yeah. Me, too. See you Monday."

I don't think Leon had a very good time. I didn't either, except for knowing I was on the first real date of my life.

I walk in the back door, my lie prepared, but immediately, I can tell something is wrong. It is totally quiet. A strange feeling comes over me.

When I go in the living room, Julian is still on the couch. He hasn't moved, except that one arm is hanging off the side, his hand touching the floor.

"Julian!" My voice echoes in the room. "Julian, wake up." His face is pale and I can't see any signs of breathing. Oh

God, is he dead? Have I killed my brother?

"Julian!" I shake him. He feels limp, like a rag doll. I try to feel for a pulse. Nothing, even though his body is warm. How long does it take to cool off? Panic grabs me in a clammy grip.

"I'm sorry, Julian. I didn't mean to. Please wake up." I run to the kitchen and wet a dish towel and wipe his face with it. His mouth is slack. I try to open his eyes, and I think I see a slight movement, but it's probably my imagination. I start to cry.

I go to the phone and call 911. They are here in minutes. They put him on a stretcher and load him into the ambulance. All the neighbors are outside, curious.

At the hospital, they ask me questions about is Julian a drug user and do I know what he took. I start to confess, tell them everything. But then something stops me.

"I don't know. Maybe some sleeping pills. Our mother had some before she died. I think they were still in the medicine cabinet."

"Do you know what kind they were?" Their voices are insistent, urgent, like the doctors on ER.

I remember the label on the bottle. "Maybe Percocet. Something like that. I'm not sure."

"Was he upset about anything? Depressed?" They think Julian has tried to kill himself. He wouldn't, but they don't know him.

"Sort of. I mean, I got a job and he was unhappy about that."

"So your husband didn't want you to work?"

"He's my brother." I almost laugh, it's so weird. "Is he going to be all right?"

"We don't know."

They send me back to the waiting room where I sit on

an orange chair, not thinking. All around me, people are talking and kids are crying. And eating. It seems like everybody in the ER is eating and drinking stuff from machines. I remember I have money in my purse. My own money. I get a Pepsi and a bag of Cheetos. Then I get a candy bar, too, a Kit Kat.

After a long time, a nurse comes out and says I can see Julian. Now I'm scared. What will I say to him?

His eyes are closed and he looks really pale and pasty white. "Hi, Julian," I whisper. He opens his eyes and stares at me.

"You tried to kill me," he says. His voice is flat, raspy, cold.

"No, Julian." I can't help it, I start to cry. "I just wanted to go on a date. I didn't mean to. It was just Mother's sleeping pills."

I grab his hand, but he shakes me off.

"You're going to jail."

"It was an accident." I hear my voice rise to a desperate, high-pitched whine.

"It was attempted murder."

"Julian, no! I'm sorry. You know I didn't mean to hurt you. You're all I've got in the whole world. Please. I'll never do it again."

"You won't have the chance, you bitch. You'll be locked up." Then he closes his eyes, shutting me out.

I can't believe how this has all spun out of control. All I wanted to do was go on a stupid date. And I didn't even have a good time. How could I have been so selfish, so dumb? I almost killed my brother, and now they're going to put me in jail. I have ruined my life.

The door opens and in walks a woman who says she is a social worker. She sits down next to Julian's bed. He opens his eyes.

She starts talking about how they are concerned about his state of mind and the resources available to people with depression. She says they will make him an appointment with a psychiatrist. I wait for him to tell her that I was the one who gave him the pills.

"Thank you," he sighs. "I have been depressed. Life just hasn't seemed worth living."

She finishes her spiel, hands Julian her card and leaves.

"You didn't tell her," I say, hardly believing it. "Thank you, Julian, thank you. I promise you it was an accident. I'll never do anything like that again. Ever, ever." I'm babbling like an idiot.

"Shut up. I just saved your ass, you bitch." I am shocked at his language. Julian doesn't usually talk this way.

"I know. Thank you, Julian. I'll make it up to you and ..."

He cuts me off. "From now on, you do everything I say. Everything. One false move and I call the police." His eyes are slitty and mean. He looks like an iguana.

I can see my life stretching ahead of me, a long desert of predictable sameness, even worse than before. It will be worse than jail. I will be Julian's slave forever. There is no hope, no light at the end of the tunnel.

Then I remember. I smile to myself. In my bathrobe pocket, there is a little container of pills. There are fourteen left. Enough.

＊

Daisy's Lament

By Nina Salley Hepburn

Question: "Will three drinks make you dizzy?"
Answer: "The price is right, but the name's Daisy."

When I first heard it, I thought that joke was made up for Daisy Lovett. It might have been.

The high school boys whispered and snickered about her, but they all had the hots for her. Quite a few bragged that they'd been to bed with her. None of us girls believed them. We laughed too, but I secretly envied her. She had a kind of cosmopolitan look that I could only dream about.

Daisy rode the bus to Lido Beach every day, it seemed. At least every time I went, she was on the bus. She always wore a leopard skin bikini. Her feet were bare except for skinny black thongs that showed off her polished red toenails.

I never saw her go into the water. She'd just spread a blanket on the sand in front of the Lido Beach Casino where we all hung out, and rub a mixture of baby oil and iodine all over her voluptuous body. As the mild Florida winter turned to spring and spring to summer, her bronze-colored skin turned deep copper.

She was taller than most women, with long slender legs. She had the biggest boobs I had ever seen on an actual person and her bikini top let them overflow in front and on the sides. Her eyes were large and brown, shaded by long thick eyelashes that looked artificial; her mouth was painted the same bright red as her fingernails and toenails. She wore her hair in a long page boy that bounced with every step she took. It was thick and dark with a hint of red. Bangs covered her forehead.

Daisy was usually alone. Sometimes, some guy would go over and sit on the blanket with her. She carried a large beach bag that matched her bathing suit and sometimes she would reach for a mirror and touch up her lipstick. On the bus, she'd read a book. Once I saw the cover. It was a John D. McDonald detective paperback. I wondered if she knew him, since he lived in Sarasota.

Did she ever go anywhere except the beach? It was a question we asked each other. And where did she live? Even though she was probably in her early thirties, we thought she was old, especially to be hanging out at the beach. Her lifestyle seemed strange beyond belief.

One night, several of us borrowed I.D.'s from older siblings and went to a bar down on Main Street. The boys had heard it was a gay bar, although we didn't call it that back then. They invited me and another girl to go check it out. We wanted to see what they did—if it was true guys danced with each other. As it turned out, we forgot to notice.

Daisy Lovett, of all people, was sitting at a small table by herself. She sipped her drink through a straw. Lenny Dee was playing keyboard and she was as close to him as she could get. She hung on every note he played, her body moving with the music. She wore short white shorts and a loose fitting Hawaiian print shirt tied high on her torso, leaving a large patch of brown skin showing in between.

She stretched her legs out toward the tiny dance floor and crossed her feet, then expanded her chest, straining the knot in her shirt.

I looked at the guys sitting at the bar. They ignored her. The three boys with us were trying to get the nerve to ask her to dance. She didn't seem to notice anything around her—except Lenny and the music.

Then it happened. She stood up and stretched her arms above her head and went into a slow seductive dance all by herself. The kind you do at home when you turn up the music and you're alone and know you won't be seen by anyone. Yet here she was in public, doing this dance.

Her hips swayed, her hands moved from side to side, then to her waist, and down around her butt. She had her back to us. She was just about two feet from Lenny. He watched her approvingly and didn't miss a beat. She turned around toward us and started to untie her shirt. Just when the boys were about to pass out, she spun around again toward Lenny and opened up the shirt, so he was the only one who could see. He smiled, his face turned red and he changed the beat of his music to what sounded like a jungle chant.

She kept dancing, doing shimmies, then faster, the shirt open, flying loose. She still faced Lenny. After a while, she tied her shirt, turned toward us and did a little bow. We all applauded, the bartender too. There was more than one wolf whistle from our group. She sat down and the barkeep brought her another drink. She smiled and reached for her money. He pushed it away and squeezed her hand.

I was a virgin. I wasn't sure about my friends. All the other girls said they were and the boys said they weren't. I suspected we all were. We knew about sex though and we talked a lot. All the way home that night, we wondered who she would sleep with—Lenny or the bartender. We never found out.

Several years later, while I was away at school, Daisy got married. I was shocked. Who would marry her? The whole town knew she was a whore, didn't they?

When I went home for the summer, I found out. His name was Donald Maris, a middle-aged man who had moved to Sarasota and opened a restaurant. She went there to eat and they met and started talking. One thing led to another and Daisy got pregnant.

I couldn't believe it. She was too old to have a baby, I thought. But she was sure pregnant and just about to pop right out of her bathing suit the first time I saw her that summer. She was on a towel, lying flat on her back, her belly looming up like a mountain. It was covered by a red and white polka dot bathing suit, but her boobs, now bigger than ever, were spilling out everywhere.

I sat close by and saw her when she left the beach. She moved as gracefully as ever in spite of her increased proportions, as she walked over to a sleek black convertible. Marriage had definitely improved her fortune.

The next summer when I came home, Daisy was pushing a baby carriage. She and her husband had bought a house in our neighborhood, and she strolled past our house every day, taking the baby for a walk. She looked happier than I had ever seen her, always smiling. She even talked baby talk walking down the street.

We had our first actual conversation that summer. I was on the front porch waiting for the postman when she sauntered by. I waved to her and she waved back and stopped, right in the middle of the sidewalk.

"Can I see the baby?" I asked, as I walked down the steps

toward her.

Her white teeth sparkled against her dark skin.

"Sure," she said. "Her name is Daisy May." She lifted the baby out of the carriage and held her out to me.

"May I?" I asked, as I accepted the plump little bundle of pink ruffles and lace. "She's beautiful." I meant it, too. Her eyes were big and brown and her lashes were almost as long as her mother's. Maybe Daisy's were actually real, I thought. Daisy May's hair was thick and dark, curled in damp little rings. Her skin was bronzed and in the lobe of each ear, she wore a tiny diamond.

"How much does she weigh?" I asked, just making conversation. I didn't really care.

"Fifteen pounds," Daisy answered with pride. "She eats everything. The doctor says she's real healthy."

The postman walked toward us and I gave the baby back.

"She's really sweet. Thanks for letting me hold her."

"Oh, it's okay," she said, "any time. In fact, maybe you could baby-sit sometime."

"Maybe," I said. I took my mail and walked back inside the house. Baby-sit? I was in college! Besides, I had a summer job at the Harbor House Cafe. And a boyfriend that I hardly had time to see. It was a cute baby and all, but no thanks, I thought, no baby-sitting.

That summer I got to know Daisy and I liked her. She didn't seem at all like we always thought she was. Not like a whore. If I was on the porch when she and Daisy May came by, they would stop and visit. Daisy May loved sitting in the porch swing.

I've thought a lot about that summer and how they were together—Daisy and Daisy May. Whatever happened, one thing's for sure. Daisy loved that baby. I for one don't believe she could have done anything to hurt her.

They came to say good-bye when I left to go back to school in the fall. We hugged and I saw tears in Daisy's eyes. Maybe I was her only friend, I thought, with a little feeling of superiority. I didn't count it as a privilege then.

By the time I came back home for Christmas break, it had happened. Daisy May had died suddenly and everyone suspected Daisy. How can that be, I wondered. Don't they know how much she loved that baby? The police investigated but the case was never solved. She wasn't arrested, but there was a cloud of doubt hanging over Daisy, and is to this day.

I wanted to call her, tell her how sorry I was, but I never did.

Before the next summer, Donald had closed the restaurant and left town. Daisy was alone again. I saw her at the beach some, but we didn't speak. I was usually with friends and she was openly picking up men. She wore even skimpier bikinis than she had before, showing off everything she could legally show.

Whoring again, I thought. Some people never change.

⊷⧓⊶

Crasher

By Beverly Williams

Nadine slips into a pew, about a third of the way from the back of the church. No one notices, or even gives her a passing glance. She looks like everyone else, in her plain navy blue dress. Gray haired, past middle age. She has settled on navy blue for funerals. When you wear black, people tend to think you're one of the family or a close friend.

There's not much of a crowd, but that's the point, of course. Every day she reads the obituaries, carefully sorting through them and narrowing the list till she finds the most worthy person. Then she goes to the funeral.

It all started when a woman who'd been her supervisor at the Internal Revenue died. Actually, the woman hadn't been all that nice to her, but Nadine felt she ought to go to her funeral as a token of respect. It was just a graveside service, and it was shocking how sparse the crowd was.

Which got her to wondering who would come to her funeral. Practically nobody. Oh, she supposed her sister would come. Wouldn't hardly speak to her, but she'd come to the funeral, just to keep people from talking. And some of her neighbors. A few of her former co-workers from the

IRS, if they could get off. And maybe some people from church, though she'd about quit going. All in all, just a handful of people.

So she started going to funerals. Not of people she knew, but of people who wouldn't have anyone. You could tell by the obituaries. Short, no illustrious career, few survivors. She felt like she was making a contribution. She privately called it her funeral ministry. Everything was a ministry these days; at her church a group of ladies had gotten together to take meals to sick people and called it the casserole ministry. It was a nice thing to do, but Nadine thought calling casseroles a ministry was a little much.

She'd thought someone might ask why she was there, or how she knew the deceased. But no one did. So after a while, she branched out and started going to other, more interesting funerals. She attended the funeral of a prominent local politician. There was a huge crowd and she recognized people whose pictures she'd seen in the newspaper. When the minister announced that everyone was invited to the home afterwards, she decided to go. She didn't stay very long, but the food was wonderful. Lots of homemade casseroles and pies. A huge platter of fried chicken. Ham biscuits. They even served drinks, although Nadine just had a cup of coffee. People acted like it was a party.

She kept on going to the sparse funerals of the people who didn't have many mourners, but she found she really enjoyed the big ones the most. Once she attended a funeral of someone who'd been murdered. The church was packed! If she hadn't gotten there early, she wouldn't have found a seat. Then she went to a Jewish funeral, because she'd never been inside a synagogue. She'd read that Jews didn't believe in heaven, and she was curious about the service. It was really nice, and no one looked at her as if she didn't belong there. She'd like to go to the funeral of a black person, but she hasn't gotten up the nerve yet. She's going to wait until a politician or some other prominent black person dies, so there will be other white people there and she won't stand out in the crowd.

Today she has decided to attend the funeral for a man who is rich and socially connected. It's easy to tell from the obituary—the Ivy League college, the bank presidency, the club memberships. It will be at an Episcopal church. Nadine admires the way the Catholics and the Episcopalians do funerals. So reverent and dignified. She wouldn't mind having that kind of send-off when it's her turn, though of course she won't.

The service is at eleven o'clock, which is good since the gathering afterwards at the house (she's looked up the address in the phone book) will take care of lunch. When the service ends, she says a special prayer for the deceased, gets in her dusty old Plymouth, and follows the procession to the cemetery. She stands near the edge of the crowd as the casket is lowered into the ground.

Then she drives to the house, which is huge, practically a mansion. She feels a spark of excitement. It is thrilling going into these big houses, seeing the kind of privileged world some people live in. So different from her own. She waits in her car until there is a large enough crowd inside for her to be unobtrusive. She has her story prepared, in case anyone asks how she knew him. She will say she used to work for his bank, murmur how he was a wonderful person. Though of course no one will ask. They never do.

As she comes in the front door, she hears the conversation, even laughter. There are so many people here, it's overwhelming. She feels like she's crashing a party. For a moment, she falters, but then she takes a deep breath and goes inside. She sees people with drinks in their hands. When a waiter passes by with a tray of filled wine glasses, she takes one, even though she considers it a bit shocking to drink in the daytime. She takes a sip and feels a pleasant little warmth as it goes down.

There is a bookcase-lined study on the other side of the entrance hall, and she goes in to look around and wait for a decent interval before she goes in the dining room where the food is. People are in there, too, talking in little conversational groups. A distinguished-looking man about her age nods to her and smiles. She smiles back. He looks vaguely familiar; she thinks perhaps she's seen his picture in the paper. She moves to the bookcase and peruses the book titles, although she's not much of a reader.

She sips her wine, beginning to feel more at ease. The man appears at her side.

"How are you today?" he asks, startling Nadine. People don't usually talk to her at funerals. Or anywhere else, for that matter.

"Fine," she says.

"I saw you at the church." Does he think he knows her? Maybe she looks like someone else.

Polite smile. She's not used to making small talk with men.

"Did you know Mr. Archibald well?"

She's thrown off guard, even though she has her story prepared. "Well … no. I … uh, worked at the bank."

"Really?" He doesn't believe her. She wonders if she should leave. But she hasn't committed a crime.

"He probably wouldn't have known me." Not that he could say anything now, of course. That was the beauty of crashing a funeral. The honoree couldn't deny that you belonged there. "But I always admired him."

"I've seen you at a number of funerals. We must know a lot of the same people."

"I suppose so."

Nadine edges away. He edges with her.

"Percy Wainwright." He smiles at her, a nice, rather shy smile.

"Nadine Upshaw." She notices how their names seem to go together, each with two syllables in the first name and two in the last. You could almost sing them.

"You know many people here?" asks Percy.

"Not very many," hedges Nadine. "Do you?"

"Not a soul," he says cheerfully. "Why don't we go in the dining room and see what the spread looks like?"

Nadine is a little hesitant about joining a stranger, but it might be better to have someone to talk to. She won't stand out as much.

"Roast beef," whispers Percy, as they near the table where a man in a white coat is carving. "Very classy. I think they had it catered."

It appears to be true. Instead of the usual casseroles and pies in an eclectic selection of platters and dishes, everything seems to go together, as if carefully planned. Nadine has never heard of a funeral being catered. It somehow doesn't seem quite as friendly. They make their way around the table and then take their plates to a quiet corner of the sun porch off the dining room.

"You should try this, Nadine," says Percy, as if they were old friends. "Crabmeat casserole. And did you get one of those little pies?"

Lemon tarts. Nadine cannot believe this elegant food. A far cry from her usual spartan lunch of Campbell's tomato soup and crackers. Sometimes a pimento cheese sandwich.

She searches for something to say. "Was Mr. Archibald a

friend of yours? Or a business associate?"

"Never met him," says Percy, taking a bite of marinated artichoke. "This is delicious. You know," he continues, "the rich really know how to do a funeral. This is the best one I've been to in a long time."

"Do you go to a lot of funerals?"

"Well, you know, when you get to be our age, lots of people die. And I rarely get invited to parties. Funerals are the next best thing." He lowers his voice. "I used to only go to funerals of people I knew. Then I decided to start picking out the good ones, you know, where they have cocktails and lots of food. I guess you could say I'm a funeral crasher." He chuckles.

"Me, too," Nadine confesses.

"I thought so. Kindred spirit." He raises his wine glass and clinks it against Nadine's. "The food helps. I don't cook much these days. But I don't just come for the food. I always go to the service and on to the cemetery, too."

"Me, too," says Nadine. "And I say a prayer for the deceased."

"Of course." They are silent for a moment. Out of respect.

"Well," says Nadine, "I guess I'd better go." When she rises, Percy does, too. "It was nice to meet you, Mr. Wainwright."

"Percy," he says. "Please. I'll walk out with you."

Nadine feels some pride at walking beside such an attractive man. She notices his tailored suit and the gold cufflinks on his crisp white shirt. She's a little embarrassed when they reach her ancient, dusty car.

"There's a funeral tomorrow afternoon I've been thinking of attending. Mimsy Caldwell. You may have read about it."

"Oh, yes," says Nadine eagerly. "That socialite who

drowned in her swimming pool. The paper said there was some question of suicide." She can't help it, it's rather titillating.

"Perhaps you would like to accompany me."

"Well ..." Nadine is hesitant. This man is a stranger, after all, in spite of his courtly manners and handsome appearance. She's always been very careful about strange men. Which is probably one reason she's single. "Maybe I'll just see you there."

"I'll look forward to it," says Percy, undaunted.

The next afternoon, Nadine finds herself dressing carefully for the occasion. She rejects the navy blue in favor of a more flattering mauve two-piece dress, a hand-me-down from her sister, Gloria. At the church, which is packed, she looks around for Percy and is disappointed when she doesn't see him. She almost doesn't go to the home afterwards, but as she is getting out of her car, she sees him coming along the sidewalk.

"Nadine," he says, "there you are." He seems glad to see her. "I was afraid you weren't going to come." He touches her elbow as they reach the front steps of the house.

Other people are coming in at the same time, and Percy smiles at them in sorrowful acknowledgement, as if to say, "Such a shame. So young."

This house is not quite as elegant as the previous one. It seems a bit neglected, although it is filled with beautiful furniture. Antiques, Nadine is sure. And lovely little pieces of crystal and porcelain. Lots of ornate silver. Things that look as though they belong in a museum.

There is a bar set up in the living room and Percy gets a Scotch and water. Nadine has a small glass of wine. They stand in a corner of the room, observing the crowd. Nadine realizes how nice it is to be with someone instead of alone.

"Are you married, Nadine?" asks Percy.

"No, never married," she says, with a self-conscious little laugh. She really hates saying that. She thinks she might invent an ex-husband. Or a dead one.

"I'm alone, too," says Percy. "My wife died last year."

"I'm sorry," says Nadine, although she's actually rather pleased to hear that Percy is single.

"We had planned to do so many things when we retired. We took one trip, and then she got sick. Lung cancer. She was gone almost before I knew it." His eyes swim and almost without thinking, Nadine gives him a sympathetic pat. Percy smiles a brave smile. "Excuse me." He disappears.

Nadine is beginning to think he's not coming back when he appears again.

"I'm sorry to be so emotional," he says. "It's just been terribly lonely."

"I understand," says Nadine. Certainly about being lonely.

"Let's check out the buffet," says Percy, cheerful again.

Afterwards, Percy walks her to her car.

"I enjoy your company, Nadine," he says, opening the door for her. "You don't know how nice it is to have someone to talk to." He looks as if he's about to cry again.

"Well, thank you, Percy."

"I brought you something." He reaches into his pocket and produces a tiny crystal sea horse. It looks quite similar to one she admired inside Mimsy Caldwell's house.

"Oh, Percy, I can't accept that. It must be very valuable."

"Not really. It's just a trinket, actually. It belonged to my wife. I know she would want you to have it. She was such a generous woman. She worried so about me being alone."

"Well ..."

"Please, Nadine." He smiles his sad, charming smile. "It

would make me happy."

It is a lovely little thing, so delicate and a pale green color. Nadine wants it. She knows the perfect place for it in her apartment, in the kitchen window that gets the morning sun.

"Thank you, Percy."

"You know, going to funerals can get a bit depressing. I thought we might go to a party."

"A party? Oh, I don't know. It's one thing to crash a funeral, but I'm not sure about a real party. Besides, I'm not exactly the party-going type."

"It will be fun," says Percy. "We'll fit right in, you'll see. I know of one tomorrow night. I'll pick you up at seven."

Nadine is apprehensive, but she doesn't want to turn Percy down. She considers buying a new dress, but she can't really afford it, so she searches her closet, and decides the dress she wore to her niece's wedding will do.

"You look lovely," says Percy when he comes to pick her up. "I have just the thing to complement that pretty dress." He holds out both his closed hands. "Pick one."

Nadine touches one of his hands. He opens it to reveal a pearl necklace. She shakes her head, flustered, and opens her mouth to protest, but Percy puts a finger on her lips.

"It's just costume jewelry," he says. "But I thought it would suit you. You're the kind of woman who should wear pearls. Turn around."

He fastens the necklace around her neck. Nadine shivers with pleasure as his fingers brush her skin.

The party turns out to be easier than Nadine expects, and much more fun than a funeral. No one seems to suspect that they are party crashers. She begins to relax and has a glass of champagne, the first she's ever had. Percy leaves to find a bathroom, and a man standing nearby makes small talk with Nadine. She begins to feel like an invited guest.

When Percy returns, he says, "It's getting late. Let's leave now."

"Just let me make a quick trip back to the buffet table. I want to get one more of those delicious little mushroom pastry things."

"No! We have to go." His tone is sharp.

Nadine picks up her purse and meekly follows him out.

"I'm sorry I snapped at you," he says, when they are at her apartment door. "It's just that I'm getting a migraine. They come on me without warning."

"That's all right," she says, relieved that he's not mad at her.

"You're so sweet, Nadine," he says. He takes her in his arms and kisses her on the mouth. Nadine feels as if she will faint.

All night long, Nadine dreams of Percy. She knows it's ridiculous to hope, but she can't help herself. She wonders if it is possible that she has finally found love. Just when she'd resigned herself, decided it wasn't going to happen for her. That's the way things work out sometimes. She tries out his name. Nadine Wainwright. Mrs. Percy Wainwright.

For the next two weeks, Nadine sees Percy almost every day. When she doesn't see him, he calls. She admits to herself that she has a boyfriend. Who would think that, at the age of fifty-four, she actually has a man of her own? And such a handsome one. Maybe it's her reward for all those years of taking care of her mother, denying herself.

She's so excited she even calls her sister, though they rarely speak. But she's disappointed. Gloria is a wet blanket, as usual.

"What do you know about this man, Nadine?" she demands. "He could be a con man. They prey on lonely women, you know."

"Oh, for pity's sake, Gloria, I don't have anything anyone would want. Besides, Percy is a perfect gentleman. You just don't want me to have anything."

It's true. Gloria has always been selfish. Always too busy with her husband and children and garden club to help Nadine take care of Mother. Then when Mother died she got half of the estate, such as it was. And had the nerve to act like she deserved it. Nadine couldn't help feeling bitter that Mother left Gloria her prettiest things, like the garnet earrings and the silver teapot.

But now she has Percy, who is so attentive and gives her lovely gifts. She makes up her mind not to be bitter any longer.

They have decided to branch out, and today they are going to a wedding. Nadine is excited. She loves weddings.

At the church, Nadine feels a surge of emotion as the bride walks down the aisle on the arm of her father. She is so lovely! She is surprised to find a lump in her throat and a tear in her eye. Percy squeezes her hand and smiles at her. She thinks maybe the wedding is giving him ideas, although she tells herself it's much too soon. Still, at their age, people shouldn't wait forever.

The reception is at the most exclusive country club in town. Gloria and her husband belong to a country club, but it's not nearly as nice as this one. White-coated waiters circulate with silver trays filled with wonderful tidbits of food and skinny little glasses of champagne. There's an orchestra and some people are beginning to dance. She hopes Percy will dance with her, although she hasn't danced in years.

Percy excuses himself for the second time. Nadine has noticed that he makes frequent trips to the bathroom, but she knows men his age have to do that. Her brother-in-law does, too. Prostate problems.

A waiter passes by and she plucks off another glass of champagne. The music picks up and the bride and groom's young friends move to the dance floor. She watches them, but keeps an eye out for Percy. He's been gone for a long time. She begins to get nervous. What if he is sick or has had a heart attack?

When she finally sees him, she feels a surge of relief. Then as he comes closer, she notices that he has a strange look on his face and his arm is held stiffly at his side. There is a man walking beside him and another behind. They are coming straight toward her. Something isn't right. Percy isn't looking at her.

They stop in front of her, and Nadine sees that Percy is handcuffed to the man next to him. The other man grabs her purse. She starts to protest, but thinks better of it. He rifles quickly through it and pulls out a wallet, a set of car keys and a Rolex watch.

Nadine is stunned. She looks at Percy, but he is looking at his shoes. People start to gather around them and their excited conversation buzzes in her ears. She is dizzy from the champagne and thinks she might faint. One of the men pulls her hands behind her back and puts handcuffs on her. They are cold and hard and they hurt her wrists.

She tries to talk to Percy as they are led outside and pushed into an unmarked police car.

"Percy," she says, her voice quavering, "what is this?"

"Percy," laughs one of the officers, "that's a new one."

"Yeah," says the other one, "what happened to Reginald? And Ian?"

"Isn't Percy Wainwright your real name?" she whispers, as the awful truth begins to seep in.

"Come on, Charlie. The least you can do is tell your

accomplice your real name."

"Charlie?"

"Charlie Scruggs," says the policeman. "Small time crook and con man."

Nadine stares at Percy. Somehow he no longer looks so distinguished. More like a Charlie than a Percy.

"I didn't know," she says. The handcuffs cut painfully into her wrists, bringing the realization that she, too, is in trouble.

"Yeah, well, they all say that. You had stolen property in your purse."

"But I didn't put it there. I swear." She's panicked now.

At the police station, they place Nadine in a cell with some very suspicious-looking women whose clothing appears to have come from one of those mail-order places that advertise in the back of magazines. Frederick's of Hollywood. They look at her and snicker; she's obviously not a member of their exclusive club.

Finally a matron comes to tell her she can leave if some-one will post her bond. All she wants to do is get out of this horrible place, home to her safe little apartment. But the thought of calling her sister almost makes her want to stay.

When her sister and brother-in-law arrive, Nadine weeps with relief. Gloria's mouth is tight with disapproval and Nadine can see her making sure she doesn't touch any sur-face in the police station.

"I told you he was a con man. But oh, no, you wouldn't listen to me. I can't believe you were so stupid! Oh, God, if this gets in the papers ... you only think of yourself, you know. You always have. Didn't it ever occur to you how embarrassing this would be to your family?" And on and on. "I'll bet that man isn't even widowed. He probably has a wife somewhere."

Nadine doesn't answer. Actually, it seems that Percy/Charlie has a number of wives. The police told Nadine that he is wanted for bigamy in Alabama, Georgia and Texas. But she doesn't want to give Gloria the satisfaction. And she's so ashamed.

When she finally gets back to her apartment, it no longer seems lonely. It seems safe. And filled with lovely gifts. She supposes she will have to give them back. She picks up the little green seahorse and cradles him in her hands.

"I'm keeping you," she whispers. She wraps him in a handkerchief and puts him in a shoebox in the farthest corner of her closet. When it's safe, she'll return him to the sunny window in the kitchen.

Nadine is cleared of the charges, thanks to the lawyer her brother-in-law hires for her. And Percy has told the police that she was innocent, for which she is grateful. Still, the disappointment and the shame are almost too much to bear. She hardly leaves her apartment for months.

Gradually, she feels better. Then one day she sees in the paper that a woman who used to live on her street has died. The woman was so nice, always asked about Mother. Nadine knows the funeral will be sparsely attended. After the service, she goes by the house, out of respect. The woman had no children and the mourners are mostly older women, like herself. Nadine has a cup of coffee and a piece of disappointingly dry coconut cake, the kind that comes from a supermarket bakery. Then she goes in search of a bathroom before she begins the twenty-minute drive back to her apartment. She's at the age where you have to take any opportunity to use the restroom.

She is passing through a bedroom on her way into the adjoining bathroom when the crystal butterfly catches her eye. It is lovely, so delicate and such a heavenly shade of blue. She picks it up to admire it. It's probably not really valuable, and she's sure no one would miss it, a little thing like that. But she knows she mustn't.

Back in her apartment, she hangs up her navy blue dress and puts on her old chenille bathrobe. She takes the little green seahorse from his shoebox hiding place in the back of her closet and carries him into the kitchen, where she returns him to the window sill.

Then she reaches into her purse and brings out the crystal butterfly. She places the butterfly next to the seahorse and admires the way the light filters through her treasures. They look lovely there, although a little lonely. She really needs another one. Maybe next week ...

❈

A Time For Sharing

By Nina Salley Hepburn

The War seemed very far away when we were kids back in 1943. There were two reminders. First, our bedtime prayers always included a plea for the War to end and the soldiers to come home safely. Second, some of our favorite things were rationed. That meant even if we had enough money, we still couldn't buy all we wanted. Like Double Bubble—every kid's favorite chewing gum.

One Saturday morning Buddy, the twelve-year-old from next door, told us that the Rexall Drug Store had a fresh supply of it. My sister Claire and I robbed our piggy banks and hurried downtown, hoping to stock up for the future. After standing in line for what seemed like hours, we finally got two pieces of Double Bubble. That would have to last us until the next shipment.

When we came home, we were surprised to find a small house trailer in the back yard. We looked it over with great anticipation. What fun we would have playing in it. Then Daddy told us what the trailer was for.

"With the war going on, there's a new Army base just

outside Dyersburg and the soldiers with families have a hard time finding a place to live. It's our duty to help out any way we can. Giving a soldier and his family a place to live is something we can do."

The Army family moved into the trailer the following Saturday and it was just about the most exciting thing that had ever happened. The soldier was tall and handsome, just like the soldiers we had seen in the picture show. His name was Billy Jamison. His wife, Sarah, was short and ordinary looking. But the most interesting thing about them was the baby, Donnie. From a distance, he looked fat and cute like other babies, but when you got up close to him, you could see the big lump on one eyelid, which ruined him as far as I was concerned. Other people would look at him and say things like, "What a cute baby. Did he bump his eye?"

Sarah would explain that it was something he was born with and when he was older, they would operate and take the lump out and he would be fine. The lump grew bigger while they lived in our back yard, but he was a happy baby, and it didn't seem to bother him.

Daddy hooked up a makeshift water line to the small kitchen in the trailer, but there was no bathroom. The Jamisons didn't seem to mind coming to ours, since it was at the back of our house. Daddy lettered a sign that could be flipped over when entering. The sign proclaimed whether the room was occupied or vacant. Claire and I were told to be considerate and make our time in the bathroom as brief as possible. He painted a thin black line about two inches long very low on the side of the bathtub and told us that was the water line. If a person used too much hot water, there wouldn't be enough for the next bath, he explained. I supposed he pointed this out to the Jamisons too, although I never heard him say it and I sometimes heard the water running for a very long time.

After a few weeks, Daddy worked out a bathroom schedule. Each person had their own time for a bath and other necessities, with free time in between. The schedule was posted on the door beside the *OCCUPIED/VACANT* sign. If someone needed to change his appointed time, he could look at the schedule, see who had the bathroom at that time, then ask to swap.

Things were going well. I was the envy of my friends. No one else had a house trailer in their back yard, much less a soldier living in it. Also, I had become quite attached to Donnie in spite of his affliction. Sarah would let me stroll him down the sidewalk afternoons after school and when people asked me about the lump, I told them just what Sarah said and no one ever asked when he would be old enough for the operation.

On the last day of school that Spring, we came home and found another surprise. The living room was completely vacant. "We've been robbed!" Claire gasped.

"I don't think so," I said, trying to reassure her. "Maybe we're getting new furniture. Daddy probably took the old stuff to the second hand store." I was trying to believe that was true. After all, with the rent from the Jamisons, there must be extra money. But when we got to the dining room, we saw that the old furniture had been crowded into one end of the room and the table and chairs moved to the other end.

We found Mother in the kitchen beating a cake with an egg beater. I could tell by the way her mouth was clamped together that it wasn't her idea to move the living room set into the dining room. Daddy obviously had a new scheme and Mother didn't like it. I had a feeling that any other subject would be safer, but somehow all I could think about was the new furniture arrangement.

"Why is the couch in the dining room?" I asked.

Mother stopped beating the cake, wiped her hands on her apron and took a handkerchief from her pocket, dabbing at her eyes up under her glasses.

"Your daddy's rented out the living room," she said. "Three more people to share the bath." She paused a minute, turning back to the cake. "I'm exasperated!"

The last time I remembered Mother using that word was when Daddy brought home a red-headed hitchhiker from Ohio and announced that he was going to stay with us until he found a job—maybe a week. Mother didn't say a word in front of the man, just smiled and set another plate on the table. When it was time to serve the stew, each portion was a little smaller than usual. But after the man was settled on the living room couch for the night, and Mother, Claire and I were doing the dishes while Daddy read the paper, Mother looked straight at him and announced, "Robert, I'm exasperated!"

Daddy put down the paper and walked over to her. "Now, honey, this poor guy's really up against it. We can help him out a little while he gets a start. He lost his job up in Ohio and hitchhiked all the way to Tennessee. He says he's a good mechanic. Even said he'd fix up that old Hudson in the garage. He wants to pay his way."

"That's another thing," Mother said. "You bought that old car when we didn't have the money. I can't even have a new living room set. Just because you met somebody who needed to sell his car, you took pity on him and bought it; and there it sits. Almost a year and never has run."

"But that's what I'm telling you. The man's a mechanic. When he gets the car fixed, I'll sell it and give you the profit. How's that now?" He gave her a squeeze and started to tickle her and soon she was laughing and Claire and I were laughing and it ended the way it always did when Mother said she was exasperated.

The man stayed more than a month and he did get the Hudson fixed before he left. I don't know what happened to the money when the car was sold. But no new furniture arrived.

This time Daddy wasn't around and I didn't know what to say.

"Three more people," I said finally. I was excited, wondering what they would be like, but I tried not to show it.

Mother had put the cake in the oven, telling Claire and me to walk carefully so it wouldn't fall, when I heard a loud roar. I looked out through the kitchen window and saw Daddy driving Mr. Randolph's pickup truck, the back end loaded with furniture. The Jamisons came out of the trailer and Billy asked Daddy if he could help with anything.

Claire and I stood in the open door that led to the back hall and watched as Daddy and Billy transformed our living room into what Daddy called an efficiency apartment. A sturdy iron bed was placed against the back wall where our couch had been. In the corner near the hall door was a small metal table with a two-burner hot plate on top and skillets and pans on the bottom shelf. Beside that stood a tall metal cabinet that someone had painted white, but at one time had been dark brown. Quite a bit of brown was still showing. Claire and I unpacked two boxes of dishes and stacked them on the cabinet shelves. A dishpan was set beside the hot plate. Two large stuffed chairs were placed near the front door with a small radio table in between.

When they had finished, Daddy thanked Billy for helping and paid him a dollar. Billy thanked him and they left to take the truck back to Mr. Randolph.

When Daddy came home, we all sat at the kitchen table and ate a piece of warm cake. "Robert, I just don't see how this is going to work out," Mother said. "There's no water in the living room. And no refrigerator. Not to mention the bathroom situation."

"Now, honey, it's going to work out fine," he said, taking a big bite of cake. "Cake's delicious, honey." It was obvious he was trying to butter Mother up. He licked his lips and handed her his empty plate. "They can get what water they need right here in the kitchen and carry it into their apartment. As for the refrigerator, well, with a little rearranging, we can easily make room for their food. It's just two people and a little boy."

"You should have discussed it with me first." She handed him another piece of cake. "It's not that I don't want to help these people out, but there is a limit. I just don't know why we have to do it all. Look at the Swansons next door. Their house is the same as ours and there's only two of them. They could take in renters a lot easier."

"Well, honey, they're old and set in their ways. They probably couldn't adjust. But we're not the only ones—lots of men at the office are renting out rooms. It's the least we can do for the war effort."

The Larsons moved in the following day. Maria looked like a movie star and talked like one, too. She sounded northern or foreign, I wasn't sure which. Her eyes were big and brown and her hair was long and shiny black. Paul Larson looked very much like Billy Jamison, tall and square and wearing the same uniform. Little Stevie looked like his mother, almost too pretty to be a boy.

The new bathroom schedule was posted and I noticed

that my bath time was now an hour earlier. When I started to run my water, I noticed too that the old line had been scraped off and a new one had been painted on about half an inch lower. If somehow Daddy should find a way to squeeze in one more family, I thought, the tub would probably be removed and only wash-ups allowed.

Often during our supper, Maria would appear in the kitchen to get supplies from the Frigidaire, or fill her dishpan. She always said "Pardon me" in her special voice and either Mother or Daddy would tell her to come on in.

We all became attached to this new family as we had to the Jamisons.

The summer was spent swinging lazily on the front porch. Sarah, Maria, Claire and I shelled butter beans and black-eyed peas for Mother to can and store for a winter of sharing. Maria and Sarah talked about the far away places they had been, like New York and Texas and California and I dreamed of going there someday. We made big freezers of ice cream; Claire and I took turns sitting on the freezer while Billy, Paul and Daddy swapped out turning the handle. A watermelon brought home by one of the men would be cut and passed around the picnic table in the back yard. It seemed we had become a family, all ten of us. Our kitchen stove, having the only oven, was almost always giving off the sweet smell of a cake or pie, cooked by Maria, Sarah or Mother and shared by all.

In the fall, when the leaves began to turn and the weather turned crisp and cool, the individual families receded into their own quarters more and more, but our way of life had been established and the sharing continued.

At Christmastime, Daddy borrowed Charlene's daddy's truck and the men drove out into the country for three Christmas trees. Claire and I helped decorate each tree with popcorn and cranberry ropes and red and green cutouts of bells, Santas and angels. Mother, Maria and Sarah cooked all during the week before Christmas and on Christmas Day we all had dinner in our dining room. Our grandparents came too and that made twelve people crowded around the table.

"This is my best Christmas," Claire said, as we dried the dishes.

"Me too," I said. "I hope every Christmas will be just like this one."

"God bless you dear girls," Maria said. "I think it's the best one for me too." She leaned over and put an arm around each of us. When I looked at her beautiful face, I saw the tears on her cheeks. Then I looked at Mother and Sarah and they were both wiping their eyes.

There were more shared meals and more happy times, but before another summer, we learned that the Army base would be closed and the soldiers stationed in Dyersburg would be transferred. It was hard for me to believe that having lived so close for almost a year, we could be flung apart, just the way we had been before the war and fate and Daddy brought us all together.

After they moved, Daddy sold the trailer and bought Mother a new living room set. He took down the OCCUPIED/VACANT sign and the bathroom schedule, but you could still see the holes where the nails had been. He scraped the black line off the tub but it was visible still when we moved out of the house years later.

✦

Backslider

By Beverly Williams

In Curtis Mayfield's opinion, there's nothing in this world better than a church picnic. And when it comes to church picnics, the hands-down best are those put on by the Cedar Grove Baptist Church. He's been looking forward to this one for a month.

He stands under a shade tree, close to the long table, watching hungrily as the ladies bring in their specialties. Curtis likes to know where the good stuff is, and what to avoid. There's Doris Vickery, setting out some low calorie casserole in a little bitty dish. No wonder Earl Vickery is so skinny—poor man probably starves to death.

"Howdy, Curtis," says Bubba Ray Blaylock, sidling up to him and nudging him with an elbow. "I figured you'd show up tonight. Bet they're missing you down at The Forty-One Club." He laughs that snorty laugh of his.

"Hell, Bubba Ray, you're down there as much as I am." The Forty-One Club is Curtis's favorite hangout, a beer joint out on Highway Forty-One.

"Not during church services, I'm not."

"I go to church," says Curtis, offended. Christmas, Easter, weddings and funerals. And the church picnic. At least he's not a hypocrite like Bubba Ray.

"Hey, Curtis, Bubba Ray." It's Mary Helen Potts. Fine looking woman, that Mary Helen. Kept her figure, unlike most of the women around here. "Y'all be sure and save some room for my lemon meringue pie."

"We sure will," they chorus eagerly.

Curtis thinks they sound like they're still in high school, when they were both in love with Mary Helen and she was in love with Ferris Potts, who she ended up marrying the day after graduation. Poor old Ferris died last year. Heart attack.

"If I wadn't married ..." says Bubba Ray.

"Yeah," says Curtis. "Me, too."

Not that he's unhappy with Frances. She's a good woman, good wife and mother. It's just that she's let herself go lately. She blames it on the menopause, which she knows is a safe excuse. Curtis isn't comfortable talking about those kind of woman things.

The Presley twins arrive.

"Howdy do, ladies," says Curtis. You can't tell them apart, with their identical home-sewn lime green pants suits and their look-alike hairdos.

"Hey, Curtis," they reply in unison.

They place their offerings on the table, edging other people's dishes over to make more room for theirs in the center. Curtis inches closer to see what they've brought. Trixie and Dixie Presley may be a little peculiar, but they are damn fine cooks. Trixie (or Dixie) has brought a meringue-topped pie that Curtis hopes is chocolate, but if it's coconut, that's all right, too. And Dixie (or Trixie) is setting out a plate of deviled eggs. One of Curtis's all time favorites, if they're made right. Mayonnaise and just a touch of mustard, no pickle. A slice of olive on top, for a crowning touch.

Nardell Sims waddles up, carrying a big coconut cake swathed in Saran wrap.

"Well, *hello*, Curtis. Nice to see *you* here." Curtis isn't sure if Nardell is being friendly or sarcastic; you never know with her. Frances says Nardell's on some kind of medication and it affects her moods.

"Hey, Nardell," he says with a smile. "That cake looks delicious."

"You be sure and get yourself some."

"I will." He'll do it just to make her feel good, but Nardell's cakes were usually on the dry side.

Curtis Junior arrives with Tammy, his sweet little wife. Junior is carrying a casserole dish, following behind Tammy like a lovesick puppy. They've just been married for a few months, and Junior looks as stoned as he did back when he was smoking that marijuana. Sex is what it is, of course. Curtis remembers.

"Hey, Daddy Curtis," Tammy says, giving him a big hug.

"Hey, honey. What did you bring?"

Curtis knows he'll have to eat some of whatever it is, which will probably be awful. Tammy grew up in a trailer park, with no daddy and a waitress mother who had a bad reputation. It's a miracle she turned out as sweet as she did. Frances is trying to teach her things, but the cooking hasn't quite taken hold yet.

The table is becoming laden now. Curtis is beginning to get a little uneasy when it finally arrives. A huge, foil-covered platter carried in by Roy Lee Tarpley, his wife Mildred walking proudly ahead. The crowd parts to let them through. Curtis detects a whiff of fried chicken. Glorious fried chicken, the queen of the church picnic. Not Colonel Sanders either. Curtis thanks the Lord for Mildred Tarpley.

She makes the best friend chicken he has ever put in his mouth. He feels like he might just pass out with desire.

"I guess y'all thought I wasn't coming," says Mildred. "I just finished frying up that chicken half an hour ago. Then I had to get dressed."

Curtis is about to pick up a paper plate when the preacher, Brother Roberts, who he's been avoiding, appears at his side.

"Nice to see you, Brother Curtis," he says. "We been missing you."

"I ... uh, I've been real busy." He shouldn't have said that. He knows there are no excuses.

"Let us pray," says Brother Roberts, in the solemn tones he uses for church.

He drones on and on. Curtis is impatient, thinking of the fried chicken getting cold. Of course, it's good cold, too, but he loves the way the crust is so crunchy when it's still warm.

"And Lord," intones Brother Robert, "bless us all, even the sinners among us. We are grateful that your bounty has brought them to us. And may they see the error of their ways. Amen."

"Amen," echoes Curtis. He stifles a snicker as he remembers the rhyme they used to say in school. Amen, Brother Ben, shot a rooster, killed a hen.

He picks up a plate and heads for the table.

⚜

Mea Culpa For Manny Roy

By Nina Salley Hepburn

I placed the tape recorder on the table beside Lucille Todd's bed and checked my watch. Ten minutes after three. "Now, when you're ready, I'll start to record. Just speak naturally. The built-in mike will pick up everything you say. If you get tired, tell me and I'll stop it. When we're finished, I'll take the tape to my office, type it up, and bring it for you to sign—say next Wednesday."

"That's too long," she said. "I'm eighty-nine years old. My kidneys are shot. I get dialysis twice a week. I might not make it 'til Wednesday."

I had never seen a person who looked so near death. The hospital bed raised her to a sitting position; pillows were packed in around her. She wore a soft yellow gown, two sizes too big, that accentuated the bony structure of her body. Her arms looked like chair spindles—her hands like hairless tarantulas. But her eyes were the worst. They were deep dark pools sunk into her angular face. Her gray hair floated from her face like a halo against the pillow, as if it were about to detach from her head. In spite of her skeletal appearance, her voice was strong and clear.

"I'll bring it tomorrow," I said.

"Good. Now, your ad in the Mountain Voice said you'd flower it up, or write it plain. I guess you better make it plain. Changing words might change the meaning. I want it clear."

"Okay," I said. I aim to please. I can write it any way the customer wants. That's what I do. I'm a writer for hire. Or in this case, a transcriber for hire. My office is in a corner of my bedroom, but I don't mention that to people who interview me. "Tell me," I said, "why now? After all these years?"

"He just died! The mean one—that told me to lie about the whole thing—I saw it in the obituaries yesterday. That's when I called you, cut out your ad two weeks ago. I been waiting all these years."

"Okay, I'm ready if you are." I said.

She nodded.

"Now if you want me to stop it, if you need to rest, just say so." I depressed the record button.

The following is Lucille Todd's story, word for word, as it was told to me on July 15, 1999:

I lied to the judge back in 1947 and I am so sorry for all the trouble it caused. I've waited all these years to fix it, to tell the truth about what happened that night in the cafe. First off, I didn't want to lie. It was them Delaney brothers that made me do it, especially that big one. Rube they called him. Said if I didn't lie he'd burn my cafe down—even kill me. Well, I never thought the marshal would go to jail—oh, maybe two years probation— something like that. What was that compared to my life? I was just about scared to death.

This is the truth, just the way it happened. Mack was a good guy. He tried to stand for the law, keep peace, you know. Every place in town served beer but me. And there was five restaurants.

Well, I tell you on a Saturday, folks would come from everywhere. I had that little hamburger joint or cafe I called it. I served plate lunches and breakfasts, and soup and chili and sandwiches, and it worked me and two girls and Gus Mabus to death. At lunchtime, we just went in a run 'til after two, and all morning on Saturdays. Everybody come out of the woodwork to town, their dogs and everything. And I'll tell you—you couldn't walk on the sidewalk. Because, the sidewalks would be so crowded that they'd walk in the streets. Wouldn't this town love to see that today?

She smiled and turned to me with the question. I nodded and she continued with her story, almost as if she hadn't interrupted herself.

It's just as dead as a doornail and I'm gonna tell you why. But anyway, back then business in Fenton was booming. Absolutely booming! 'Course, we sold a hamburger for a dime. You can imagine how rich we got. You know what I paid my girls?

I shrugged my shoulders and made no comment. I knew she would answer her own question.

Twenty-five cents a hour. And they was glad to get it. You know Izzard County was wet then but after what happened, they voted it dry and the place just kind of died. And that's the truth of it.

Anyway, that night I saw 'em come in. There was three of 'em. And he wasn't drinking—the one that got killed. The others was, and you know, I had the only place in town that didn't serve beer. They had already made the rounds, and they had been every place, I guess, and sopped up all the beer they could and then come in my place to eat and the oldest one and the next to oldest one was—oh, they was so drunk. The young one wasn't and he was telling them to quiet down, that I was a nice person and not to cause no trouble. But they made all kinds of noise and such language you never heard. Oh, I wanted to shut my ears.

Well, here come Mack Roy. Broad-shouldered and handsome, with those dark blue eyes that kind of danced when he smiled at you. He was the marshal, you know, and I think he had warned them if they didn't quiet down, he was gonna run them out of town.

Well, they was sitting at the end booth and well, I was trying to serve them and I had one of the girls that worked for me, and I asked her to stay with me, cause it was beginning to get late in the evening and the café was still hopping. And so, in come Mack with a big smile on his face. And he said, 'I told you all that if you didn't quiet down, I was gonna run you out.' Not mean or nothing. Just said it like that, kind of soft and still smiling.

And the old big one, Rube, he just reached up and hit Mack. For no reason! Then it was a free for all. Mack, he kept telling me to get out, and they was, well you see, I had two booths and then my counter. Four seats on each side, and they was fighting right there in the front in the aisle, and these other customers got up and jumped across the counter and ran out the back door. And Mack kept saying, 'Get out, Lucille, get out.'

Well, I run out the back and then I thought about my money, and I went back in there and grabbed it. I was rushing out the back door with my money bag. They was fighting, and then they was trying to get the gun away from Mack, and so he pulled his gun out and he was trying to get the bullets out of it. And he fired, not at them, but he fired, and he thought I was out the back door. The bullet went through the booth and the wall and through the kitchen door and through my leg. And then they finally got it away from him and beat him over the head till he was pitiful looking.

Mack didn't shoot nobody a' purpose and that's the honest-to-God truth. In all the hubbub, that boy got shot. So then they went out, the ole big one and the other one, and they walked up and down in front of the cafe, and the big one stood outside and run his hand through the window. He was so drunk he didn't know what to do, cut his arm, blood was flowing everywhere They come back in, dragged their brother out, laid him on the sidewalk.

Well, by that time, I had got out the back. I looked down and the blood was running down my leg. 'I believe I'm shot,' I said to nobody. I was so scared! That was the most awful thing I've ever been through, and I could hardly walk for the bleeding. But I made it down to the drugstore, which was next door to the pool hall. The pool hall was next to my place.

And I went in the back door, and Mr. Hamer—he was the druggist—looked at my leg and told me I should go home, and he took me home. And by that time, I was in a nervous chill. It took my son and my husband to hold me down, and then Dr. West come up to see about me. And he had to give me a shot, I remember. And he dressed my leg.

Dr. West said the bullet just went right through my leg. And he told me it was a good thing it went through like it did, cause if it had a' got that big artery, I'd been dead before they could a' got me to the hospital. And then I sort of had like a nervous collapse, 'cause I shook and perspiration was just running down my arms and rolling off, and then I just went into a nervous fit. I know now I was in shock. Back then I didn't know nothing about that sort of thing.

Then Mack come up to the house while Dr. West was still there. To see about me. Dr. West had to take him down to his office and tend to him. 'Cause they beat him over the head, just to a pulp. Pistol whipped him. He told me they bent the trigger guard, they just beat him so hard. That's why he emptied his gun. He knew they'd kill him. And Mack didn't mean to hurt nobody.

With all them fighting and everything, they throwed dishes, they broke my window. They tore up the cafe. And there was blood everywhere. I wasn't even able to get out of bed next day and my husband went down there. And Gus Mabus. He was a little half-witted, but he helped me around the cafe and I fed him. It took him and the two girls that worked for me and my husband to get the place cleaned up and opened by lunch.

Well, I was still in the bed, and those Delaney brothers came to see me. That big one, Rube, did the talking. 'We're real sorry about you getting hurt, Mrs. Todd, but our little brother's dead. All we want is for you to tell the truth. That the marshal came in there to get us—to make trouble. We weren't doing nothing. Mack just went crazy—started shooting. Your cafe got tore up, you got shot in the leg, and our brother got killed. Murdered in cold blood.'

I went into one of those nervous fits, and water started pouring off of me and it took me a long time to get over it. 'But, but,' I said. 'The marshal was just emptying his gun. He didn't mean to hurt nobody.'

'Our brother's dead, Mrs. Todd,' he said, and he leaned real close to me. I felt his hot breath in my face and smelled the whiskey. 'We don't want no more people dead—or places burned down or nothing bad happening to nobody.'

I knew that was a threat and I didn't want to die!

Before they left, Rube said, 'Now you know what to say, Mrs. Todd. The D.A. will be coming around to talk to you. And there'll be a trial. You'll have to testify. Do you have any questions 'bout what you're supposed to say?'

I was so nervous I could just barely whisper, but I said no. I knew what I had to do.

'Hope you get better soon,' the younger one said. 'Just remember—our little brother is dead—murdered by the marshal.' I was shaking so bad, I had to have Dr. West come give me another shot.

They even hired their own lawyer. Brought him to the cafe one time and told me to get a cup of coffee and come over at the booth and talk to them. That was before the trial, and they wanted to make sure I knew what to say.

Well, by then, I had already talked to the D.A. and told him what they wanted me to say. I felt so bad about Mack, who was out on bail and I'd see him around, looking pitiful. He didn't stand up tall and straight no more. His shoulders kind of rounded over and he was wearing some old plaid shirt and jeans. He didn't look right without his uniform. Out of a job and all, 'til after the trial was over, but he was out on bail. He didn't come into the cafe, but I'd see him walking by and he'd look at me, through the window, those big blue eyes just burning holes in my skin. I guess he knew what I was about to do to him.

And, so then the trial come up, and poor Mack. He told the story just like it happened. And I was the witness against him. I lied—to save my hide. He stared at me during the trial and I couldn't look at him, 'cause I knew he was innocent. But I thought he'd get maybe two years, maybe probation, if they even thought he was guilty.

Well, the jury believed me and those Delaney brothers. They found him guilty of second degree murder and he got twenty-five years in the pen.

I wanted to stand up there in the courtroom and shout. 'He's not guilty of murder. It was all a accident.' But I didn't. The Delaney brothers was watching me, so I kept my mouth shut and watched the sheriff handcuff Mack and take him away.

After the trial, those brothers put a big tombstone on the young one's grave. Bold as you please. 'Murdered in cold blood, by Mack Roy, Marshal of Izzard County.'

They let Mack out on good behavior after sixteen years and he come back to Izzard county. His grandmother had died and left Mack a little farm out at the edge of Fenton. So he stayed there. It wasn't hardly worth having, nothing but hills and rocks, but it was a place to stay. Way before then, his wife had divorced him and took his little boy away from here. It was so sad 'cause he was crazy about the kid. Called him Manny and he looked just like Mack. Used to bring him to town and they'd be holding hands, walking down to the ice cream store, big ole smiles on their faces. I don't know if he ever saw the boy again.

Mack was a different man from the one that I knew back then. Lots of people said he was plumb crazy. He'd walk to town mumbling to himself. Sometimes he'd stop in the middle of the street, pound his walking stick in the pavement, then turn around and walk right out of town. He didn't make no sense at all. He had turned into a old man in prison—and crazy too.

The Delaney brothers was still around too, but I never saw them anywhere near Mack. About ten years ago, the next to the oldest one got hit by a train and died. They said he was drunk. The next year Mack died. We had never spoke a word since it happened. But Rube was still around and he was the one I was scaredest of.

I always wanted to tell the true story. My conscience has kept me from sleeping a good night all these years. Now that Rube's dead and I'm dying, I'm telling it. I'm doing it for Mack's boy, Manny, wherever he may be, seeing as how it's too late to help Mack. That and to set the record straight.

That Delaney boy was not murdered in cold blood. And that's the truth. They was all wrestling over Mack's gun. He was trying to empty the bullets out, because they was taking it away from him and he knew that he had to, and he said, 'Lucille, get out, get out.' And he thought I was out and he started emptying it, the only way he could—shooting it—and them trying to take it away from him. He didn't know where the bullets was going. And one happened to hit the boy in the stomach. And the other one went through the booth and through the door and you know, ricocheting here and there and it just happen I come back in to get my money. It left a hole in the booth, and the wall and the door and my leg.

She motioned for me to stop the recorder. "That's it," she

said. "I'll sign it tomorrow when you come. Now, when I die, which may be any day, I want you to take it to the Sheriff. I'll pay you what we agreed—half today and the rest tomorrow."

She handed me the crisp new bills. I saw a brightness in her sunken eyes that I had not seen earlier. She smiled a weak smile and thanked me, holding onto my hand. I squeezed her hand, told her good-bye and left.

At three the following afternoon, a nurse stopped me on the way to her room. "Are you Miss Philpot?" she asked, and I knew.

"Yes," I whispered. I hoped I was wrong.

"Mrs. Todd expired during the night," she said. "She gave me this after you left yesterday. Said if anything should happen to her, I was to give it to you." She handed me a small change purse.

Inside was the money she owed me and a note, reminding me of my instructions. I left the Pine View Nursing Home and went directly to the sheriff's office. Then I went to the cemetery where the Delaney boy was buried and found the tombstone. It stood tall like a beacon in the center of the Delaney family plot. Big and bold, those condemning words jumped out at me: 'Todd Delaney, age 19, Murdered in cold blood, by Mack Roy, Marshal of Izzard County.'

I wanted to take a sledgehammer and smash it to bits. Would that help make up for what happened?

The sheriff has tried to find Manny Roy, but so far, no luck. Maybe if Lucille Todd's story is told ....

Manny Roy, wherever you are, this is for you. I hope you read it and I hope it brings you peace.

Hotsy Totsy

By Beverly Williams

Our family wasn't fancy and no one could say we were snobs, but we had our standards. We were conservative, hard-working, law-abiding people, church-going for the most part. The kind folks in Mississippi describe as salt of the earth.

Mama had three sisters and one brother, and the women formed the core of the family. Sort of like the board of directors of a company. Of course, there was Daddy's family, and the various in-laws who married in, but there was no doubt who ran things. Mama was the CEO and her mother, my grandmother Minnie, who lived next door to us, was the chairman of the board.

Uncle Billy Ray was Mama's baby brother, and everybody adored him. He was good-looking and kind of wild, but more fun than anybody. I remember hearing lots of talk about him sowing wild oats, although I didn't know what that meant at the time.

"Billy Ray better watch out, sowing all them wild oats," Daddy would say. "He might be harvesting him a crop of little bastards."

"Hush up, Mac," Mama would hiss, cutting her eyes in my direction. "Little pitchers."

Every time she said that, the flow of interesting conversation got cut off.

When Billy Ray announced that he was getting married, everybody was kind of surprised, but happy he was settling down at last. Until they learned that the bride-to-be was Totsy Vine.

The Vine family was just about the worst in the whole county. They were shiftless at best and larcenous at worst. Quite a few of them were alumni of the state prison at Parchman. The older Vines traveled around in ancient pick-up trucks or old wrecks of cars with souped up engines, while the younger generation terrorized the population on huge, scary motorcycles. The few of them that worked made their living by bootlegging or running crap games; the rest of them just stole. Some of them were on welfare. All the Vine women had bad reputations, whether they deserved them or not, although they generally did. About the only thing they had going for them was good looks. Almost without exception, the Vines were eye-popping, traffic-stopping good-looking.

When Billy Ray announced that he and Totsy Vine were getting married, Grandmother was so shocked she couldn't say a word and Mama was furious.

"I knew something like this was going to happen," she said, banging the pots and pans in the kitchen. "Running around with those Vines. I just can't believe he would actually marry that … Totsy."

"Honey, we don't even know her," Daddy said. "Maybe she's a nice girl."

Mama shot him a look. "She's a Vine." As if that said it all.

The family selected a delegation to have a talk with Billy Ray, but when they got to his house, it was too late. He and Totsy had driven over to Georgia and gotten married the night before.

Well, there was nothing to do but make the best of it. Billy Ray was a grown man, thirty-two years old, and nobody could tell him what to do. He was family, after all, and everybody loved him. If he was happy, we were going to be happy for him. Mama and Grandmother and the aunts quickly hustled up a dinner to celebrate the marriage and welcome Totsy into the family.

It was summertime, which was a good thing, because there would be at least thirty people there, counting kids, and we needed to overflow onto the porch and into the yard. Family gatherings were always pot luck affairs, with everyone bringing their favorite dishes. Daddy would start barbecuing a pork shoulder at about dawn, and as the clan arrived, the men would gravitate to the barbecue pit, where they would stand around and tend the fire, offering suggestions and drinking beer and talking politics. Mama and the women were in the kitchen, and the kids went in all directions. This time everyone got there early, anticipating the arrival of Billy Ray and his new bride, Totsy. No one knew what her real name was.

"Here they come," yelled my cousin Bo, the unofficial lookout. Billy Ray's red convertible was stirring up dust coming up our driveway, rock and roll music blasting.

Mama and the other women scurried out of the kitchen, drying their hands on dish towels and whipping off aprons.

Billy Ray roared to a stop under a tree and jumped out of the car. The kids swarmed toward him like he was the Pied Piper, then dropped back shyly as he opened the door for Totsy. The grown-ups gathered around.

"I want y'all to meet my bride," said Billy Ray, beaming like he'd just married a fairy princess. "This is Totsy."

Totsy Vine Walker was something to behold. She had long red hair, wind-whipped into a wild tangle, a creamy complexion with only maybe half a dozen pale freckles, and a wide, sexy mouth like Julia Roberts. When she unfolded her long legs to get out of the car, every male, man and boy, gasped for breath. Not only did Totsy have fantastic legs, every inch of them was on display. She was wearing the shortest, tightest shorts I'd ever seen, the kind Mama would never in a million years have let me wear. Her halter top revealed a butterfly tattoo on her shoulder. Grandmother looked like she was fixing to faint dead away and you could almost hear the hum of disapproval from Mama and the aunts.

I looked at Mama, whose mouth was in a straight, tight line. I knew that look. But she took a deep breath and marched right up to Totsy.

"It's nice to meet you, Totsy," she said. "Welcome to the family."

"Thank you for inviting me," said Totsy. It sounded as if she'd rehearsed it.

Billy Ray put a protective arm around her and led her from person to person, introducing her to everybody in the family. He got a beer and one for Totsy, too. Most of the women in the family didn't even drink beer, and if they did, they poured it into a glass. Totsy drank hers right out of the can. I thought she looked very cool.

I hung around and watched them for a while. Billy Ray looked at Totsy like she was strawberry shortcake with whipped cream on top. She kept her arm around him with her hand tucked into the back pocket of his jeans, like she wanted to be sure he didn't get away.

After a little while, Daddy sent me into the kitchen to tell Mama and the aunts that the barbecue was ready. The women were buzzing.

" ... absolutely *poured* into those shorts."

" ... up to her you-know-what."

" ... a real Hotsy Totsy all right."

They all laughed at that. I could tell poor Totsy was going to have a hard row to hoe. Like I said, Mama and them ruled the family. If they'd had any say-so in it, Totsy Vine would never have become a Walker.

But they were polite, and the men made a big point of congratulating Billy Ray and doing a lot of laughing and rib-nudging. They looked at him like he'd just won the jackpot at one of the casinos up in Tunica.

Even though Totsy looked like a movie star, she seemed kind of shy. She didn't say much to anybody except Billy Ray and she stayed right by his side all night, most of the time with her hand in his back pocket. Even when supper was over and all the women flocked back to the kitchen to clean up, Totsy stayed with Billy Ray and the men.

Later that night, after everybody had gone home, I heard Mama and Daddy talking.

"I could just wring Billy Ray's neck," said Mama. "All the women who would have given their eye teeth to marry him. That sweet little Cynthia Branch was crazy about him. And Mabel Whitworth's daughter Becky—she would have been perfect. But no, he had to up and marry a Vine. He should have known she wouldn't fit in."

"You got to admit she's good-looking," said Daddy.

"Good and trashy looking," said Mama. "Doesn't she have any sense? Coming to meet your new in-laws looking like a streetwalker."

"Well, it was a picnic. Maybe she thought that 's what she

was supposed to wear."

"For heaven's sake, Mac, what's the matter with you? You're not any better than Billy Ray. I tell you one thing, it'll never last."

"I don't know, hon. I think Totsy's gonna keep Billy Ray pretty damn happy."

I guess she did, because every time we saw them, they both looked more in love than ever. But Totsy kept coming up with new things for the women to criticize. Her clothes, for one thing.

"I don't know where on earth she finds those tacky outfits," said Aunt Jensy.

"She orders them out of a catalog. Frederick's of Hollywood," said Mama's cousin Suellen, in a triumph of new information. "I asked her."

"You know where they're going on vacation? Graceland," Mama snorted.

"I think it's just disgusting the way she hangs on Billy Ray all the time. With her hand in the pocket of his jeans. It's downright obscene." This from Aunt Brenda.

Their private nickname for her was Hotsy Totsy, which always brought chuckles from them. When she was around, they were polite to her, but they didn't cross the line into acceptance.

But the thing about Totsy that made her really intolerable was that she just didn't seem to care. Didn't realize she was trailer trash who'd married herself into a better class of people. If she'd been meek and humble, Mama and them would have stifled their distaste for her tacky background and set about the task of molding her into a reasonable facsimile of the kind of wife they had in mind for Billy Ray. But, no. She treated everyone with a kind of off-hand good humour, but when it came to being accepted by them, it was clear that she "didn't give a shit," to put the matter in Totsy's vernacular.

The men in the family seemed to like her a lot. She drank beer and laughed at their raunchy jokes and flirted just a little, but she always stayed close to Billy Ray.

"She's a good sport," said Daddy. "Y'all ought to make more of an effort to get to know her."

"We have," said Mama, but I didn't think that was exactly true. Totsy was an outsider and it looked as if she was going to stay that way.

Then my grandmother got sick and everybody kind of forgot about Totsy.

Grandmother Minnie, whose real name was Minerva, lived by herself in the house next door to ours. Even though she had gray hair and her skin was mapped with fine wrinkles, she seemed ageless to me. We loved her, of course, but she was kind of intimidating. Tall and straight and dignified, not soft and cuddly like my other grandmother. Given to quick, businesslike pats instead of hugs and kisses.

"You children should take better care of yourselves," she'd say whenever someone came down with a cold. "Look at me. I've never been sick a day in my life."

Until she developed a persistent cough and the doctor diagnosed her with cancer. She refused surgery and chemotherapy, deciding instead on a course of willpower and prayer.

Family, friends and neighbors rallied round and there was a steady stream of traffic in and out of the house next door. Bearing casseroles and flowers and offers to stay with her, but she'd never let anyone stay. She said she was fine. Billy Ray came by every night when he got off work, and Totsy was always with him.

Early one morning I went over with Mama to fix

Grandmother's breakfast and there was Totsy, sitting in the living room, drinking a Dr. Pepper and painting her fingernails. You could tell Mama was shocked.

"Oh ... Totsy," she said. "Where's Billy Ray?"

"He went home to get some sleep," said Totsy. "Miss Minnie wasn't feeling too good, so I stayed with her all night."

"You should have called me," said Mama. She never liked being left out of any decision, no matter how small.

"Oh, we didn't need you. Me and Miss Minnie got along fine."

You could almost see the steam coming out of Mama's nose and ears, she was so ticked off, but Totsy didn't seem to notice.

"It was very nice of you to stay, but I'm here now. You can go home." I thought Mama was being kind of rude myself. The words were okay, but there were icicles in her voice.

"Okay," said Totsy cheerfully. "I'll just go tell Miss Minnie goodbye." Well, there wasn't anything Mama could say about that.

The whole Grandmother Minnie situation developed into a kind of cold war between Mama and Totsy, but the interesting thing was that Totsy didn't even seem to know it. I overheard Mama talking to Billy Ray, trying to be diplomatic.

"We really don't need Totsy around all the time," she said. "The rest of us can take care of her."

"Mom likes to have her there," said Billy Ray. "She says Totsy cheers her up."

Then one day we went over to Grandmother's and heard laughter coming from the bedroom. When we followed the sound, there was Totsy lounging on Minnie's bed, leaning against the footboard. The two of them were giggling like teenagers. Mama's mouth got tight in that way it does.

"What's so funny?" she said, in a suspicious voice.

"Oh, Totsy was just telling me this hilarious story about her uncle George Vine. Grape, we used to call him." She wiped tears from her eyes with a corner of the bedsheet.

"I'm surprised you knew Totsy's uncle."

"Oh, I knew him all right. Pretty well, as a matter of fact. I tell you, that boy was some kind of good-looking." She got that faraway look in her eyes that old people get when they're remembering something good.

"I guess I better be going," said Totsy. She swung her long, shorts-clad legs off the bed in one languid motion. "See you tomorrow, Miss Minnie."

"Bye, honey," said Grandmother. She rarely called anyone honey.

"I don't know why Totsy insists on hanging around you," said Mama, when Totsy was out of earshot. "If she's bothering you, just let me know, and I'll tell her. Nicely, of course."

"Let her stay," said Grandmother. "She's good company. Doesn't look so down in the mouth all the time like everybody else."

"Fine," huffed Mama. "If that's what you want." I guess her feelings were hurt, and maybe she was kind of jealous, too.

"I think my mother is losing her mind," said Mama to Daddy that night. "Letting that Totsy stay there all the time. I went over there this morning and there that girl was, sprawled all over the bed. Wearing shorts in November. She even had her shoes on. And Mother not saying one word about it."

"I guess Miss Minnie likes her," said Daddy. "She is her daughter-in-law."

"That's not the same as a daughter," insisted Mama. "Anyway, if she wants to be so helpful, she ought to go home and cook a hot meal for Billy Ray. Instead of living on pizza all the time."

"Now how do you know that?" Daddy sounded like he thought the whole thing was funny.

"I just know it. She's not the cooking type."

Well, it went on like that for months. Totsy kept coming to Grandmother's house every day like it was an oasis in the desert. When Grandmother got weaker and everybody knew it was close to the end, they all started tiptoeing around and speaking in soft voices.

Not Totsy, though. She would blow into the house like a rowdy wind. Mama said she had no sense of what was appropriate.

"Hey, Miss Minnie," she'd yell, ignoring Mama's frown of disapproval. "I brought you a banana split from the Dairy Queen. You better eat it before it melts."

"Just what I've been craving," said Grandmother, her voice weak.

"Mother, if you'd told me, I would have been glad to get you a banana split," said Mama.

"I didn't know I wanted one," said Grandmother. "It's like Totsy read my mind."

I was sorry for Mama, I guess, but I liked Totsy myself. She talked to me like I was her age, and she let me paint my toenails with her nail polish, a shade called Passion Plum. When Mama saw it, she made me take it off.

Grandmother Minnie died in February, in her own bed, just like she wanted to. She orchestrated the whole thing, the way she had in life. She had a long talk with the preacher about her funeral, then she had everybody in the family come in, one at a time, for a private audience. Even me. And even Totsy. Mama was last, because she was the oldest. When she came out, her eyes were red and she didn't say anything.

Then Grandmother just closed her eyes and left, like she was going somewhere else. I pictured her floating up to a technicolor Heaven, where I figured she'd immediately take over and run things, just the way she had on Earth.

The day of the funeral was one of those cold, damp days we have in the South in February, when the clouds hang low and it looks like it's going to snow but nothing happens. The Methodist Church was packed. All the family was sad, but Billy Ray was taking it the hardest, him being the baby and all. Mama was on one side of him, patting his shoulder, and Totsy was on the other.

Totsy had on a black dress, lacy, short and low cut. I was expecting to hear Mama and the aunts whisper something about appropriate funeral attire, but nobody said a word.

When we got back to the house after the funeral, the women headed straight for the kitchen, where they put aprons on over their dark dresses and began assembling the food that had been arriving for the past two days. Ham and fried chicken, casseroles and cakes, pies and rolls. People would be coming to the house for the traditional funeral buffet.

"Here," said Mama to me, "put these forks on the table."

Then, with a determined stride, she marched over to where Totsy stood off to the side, with her arm around Billy Ray.

"Totsy," said Mama, "we need you in the kitchen."

Totsy looked like she was fixing to faint. She gave Billy Ray a plaintive look before she removed her hand from the back pocket of his suit pants and followed Mama into the kitchen. She stood still as Mama plucked an apron off the hook on the wall and tied it around Totsy's waist. It hung below the hem of the black lace dress.

Mama gave Totsy's shoulder a little squeeze. Then, as if by unspoken agreement, the aunts and the other women enfolded her into their midst.

"Come on, honey," said Aunt Jensy, "help me put these finger sandwiches on Minnie's good china platter."

Totsy's face was suddenly transformed. Somehow she didn't look beautiful but trashy any more; she just looked beautiful. With the conferring of an apron, Totsy Vine was accepted into their exclusive sorority. She was now a member of the Sisterhood Of Women Who Do What Needs To Be Done.

We never knew what changed things. Maybe it was something Grandmother Minnie said to Mama before she died. But from that day on, Totsy was a true member of the family. Oh, she was still Totsy and Mama was still Mama. Totsy still drank beer straight from the can and when she showed up in one of her Frederick's of Hollywood specials, displaying a little too much bosom and leg, you could still see Mama's mouth get tight. But she brought a certain panache to our family and over the years we came to depend on her kind heart. She learned to make a few casseroles with mushroom soup and she and Billy Ray produced two beautiful and surprisingly well-mannered children. After a while, we Walkers wondered how we ever got along without our own Hotsy Totsy.

❈

For the Love of Oz

By Nina Salley Hepburn

The room is totally dark and still.

There is no concept of time and place—no familiar neon numbers on the cable box—yet I am in a panic, as if I've been running for my life. My heart races. I feel sweaty, but cold. I can barely move, let alone run.

I shiver, pull the covers tighter to me, realizing it is the cold that woke me up. Of course. Power off, heat off. The video clock is dark. I fear something unseen—I don't know what. I reach across the cold sheet to touch Oz. Not to wake him, just touch him. I need the reassurance of his presence. But the familiar warmth that usually radiates from his body is missing. I inch closer and reach farther over across the king-size bed. Then I realize—he's not there. Don't get hysterical, I tell myself. He could be in the bathroom. Lately he's been getting up during the night occasionally. Not like me— two or three times a night—but sometimes once. I listen and wait. But there is no sound.

Then, after some minutes, I hear the soft whisper of wind in the distance. A whoosh, really. Oh, God! I feel in the drawer beside my bed until my hand is on the flashlight. Oz gave it to me years ago. "Keep it in your nightstand in case of an outage." There is one on his side of the bed too. I flip the switch and illuminate the bedroom, aiming the light stream at Oz's side of the bed. It is untouched—his pillow has no indentations from his head resting on it. The covers not even turned back or rumpled. He hasn't been to bed at all! Where can he be? My mind reaches back to bedtime. Did I come to bed first? Usually *he* does, but I can't remember.

I throw off the covers and grab the old wooly robe I keep in a chair nearby during winter; then make my way slowly down the stairs, holding onto my beacon of light with one hand, the stair rail with the other.

When we moved here twenty-two years ago, we didn't give a thought to stairs. I'd run up and down them fifteen or twenty times a day. Oz too. Now he drags himself up, holding onto the rail like a lifeline. We've had the handyman tighten it twice already. It's loose again.

Those were our dancing days, the glory days when we were honeymooners. We met late in life actually. Both of us alone, I more than Oz, because he still had his children even though they were grown and living on their own. I had lost my one child—along with my husband of twenty-five years. For years I grieved. I was a grieving machine, living and working in a haze of fog that I surrounded myself with in my effort to keep the world around me at a distance. I'd never get close to another person, I thought. I went to the bank every day, counting other people's money, greeting people, smiling pleasantly pretending I didn't have a care in the world. Then three days a week I went to see Dr. Cox— my therapist, my salvation.

Downstairs now. Breathless again. I flash my light around the living room and watch the shadows on the wall—lamps and pictures dancing eerily.

I call out to him, as I go from room to room. "Oz ... Oz ..."

There is no answer. In the kitchen I search for candles and matches. Standing there rifling through cluttered drawers I notice a draft around my ankles. I aim the beam at the back door. It is ajar! Dear God! That's the whoosh I heard upstairs. How did it happen? Didn't we each check every night to make sure the doors were securely locked? Had we both forgotten? I strain to recall the order of things last night—if it in fact is now morning. It must be, because I feel wide awake and it seems a long time since I went to bed. So long I can't call to mind going, no matter how I try. Yes, it has to be morning. What has happened to Oz?

I open the door a bit more—letting in cold wind—shine the light out over the patio, then slam the door and lock it. Wait a minute. What if Oz is out there somewhere wandering? Do I really mean to lock him out? But what would he be doing stumbling around in the dark? And why? Oh, God, why? He might have fallen, could be hurt and lying on the ground crying, unable to get up. He was never a strong man even when we first met. Oh, he could twirl me around the dance floor—he was smooth and graceful. But when it came to physical work or lifting heavy objects, he'd call someone else. If I wanted to rearrange furniture, he liked it the way it was. If I insisted on moving something more than a few inches, he'd offer to call his son Donald to come over.

And he's become worse. We don't dance anymore—I've lost my stamina as well, but he lost his first. It's o.k. with me—I settled easily into my "rocking chair" role with no regret. Retirement suits us both just fine.

He began crying after his prostate surgery a few years ago. It nearly broke my heart to see him hurting so and I held him in my arms. Ever since, he seems to cry as easily as I do. Sometimes we sit on the couch and watch an old movie on TV—both of us sniffling. Oz used to try to hide his sentimentality, but not any more. We hold hands and cry together. I love him for it.

Now I picture him lying on the ground unable to get up, crying out for me. Tears form in my eyes and run down through the crevices of my face.

I have to find him.

Go upstairs, get dressed. Then look for him. But first— my watch. I need to know what time it is. The clock on the stove is dark. The wall clock that belonged to my grand- mother has to be wound with a key and I sometimes forget to do it. Instinctively, I light it up. Of course the pendulum is still, the hands read six o'clock. The key is nowhere to be seen. My watch is the only hope, but where is it? I try to remember—I do this all the time. Oz tells me to keep it in one place when I take it off, but I'm not always in the same place. I search everywhere downstairs. Perhaps I left it upstairs. I need two watches, like my two pairs of glasses. That would save me a lot of trips up and down. Oz would know what time it is. He only takes his Timex off to show- er, then puts it back on before leaving the bathroom.

I haul myself upstairs, thinking about when I last climbed these steps. When I went to bed and where Oz was then— still trying to remember. I find my watch on the table beside my bed. It's four fifteen. Two more hours 'til daylight. My flashlight starts to dim. I walk around to Oz's side of the bed and pull out his drawer. I'll use both flashlights outside. I shine the light on his pillow, still fluffy, pick it up and hug it to me, smelling the essence of him. I abandon the idea of getting dressed, only slide my feet into my rubber boots and pull my robe tighter around me. I need to hurry.

The darkness hangs on like a heavy blanket. It's especially dark without the glowing automatic fixtures that surround our complex. And there is no moon tonight. I've never been outside alone in the dark but I'm not afraid. I don't even think about fear—just about Oz. A fleeting thought slips into my mind. *This is what life is like without him.* I won't accept it, can't let myself think it. Not yet.

The wind whips through my fleece robe and flannel nightgown sliding across my skin like an icy sheet. *We're in a canoe again, the late fall breeze biting me. We hit a rock with the front tip of the boat and roll slowly over, dumping us both into the freezing water. My life is over, I know for sure, and I'm no longer cold. I'm dead. I fight at first trying to find the top—reaching for air. Then my head hits something hard and I give up, inhaling the clear river water. When I'm dizzy and almost gone, something is pulling me, dragging me through the water, and then I'm on the bank coughing up water, choking and gasping. I am shaking uncontrollably and then there is a gentle hand on my face and a warm kiss. I relax a bit. "Thank God you're alive," I hear him say. "I love you, Katy B." I feel a blanket spreading over me and hear voices all around—excited, relieved, curious. I say a silent prayer to God for giving me Oz.*

My friend Margie talked me into going to the dance where I met him. I hadn't danced since I was young and didn't even remember how. Tony and I had not danced during all the years of our marriage. But I still missed him every day and the thought of being in a man's arms was frightening.

"We'll go home whenever you're ready," Margie said.

As it turned out, I wasn't the one who wanted to leave.

Now I smile, in spite of being chilled to the bone and afraid, thinking about Oz, and the way he approached me. He walked from across the room over to our table right straight to me. Margie and I were sitting at a table with several other women.

"My name is Oslo Northern," he said. "May we dance?"

I looked around at the other women, waiting for someone else to stand. No one did.

"I'm asking you," he said as he reached for my hand.

I let him help me up without speaking. Shaky as I was, he seemed to have us gliding around the dance floor in seconds—to the tune of "Lost in the Fifties." The song itself brought back memories long forgotten and his hand on my back seared through my blouse to my skin. Surely everyone could see the flush in my face.

"You dance well," he said, lying. "Your name is?"

"I'm sorry." Where had my manners gone? "Thank you, but I haven't danced in years. My name is Kathryn." For some reason, I blurted out the rest. "Kathryn Beatrice Collins.

"And what do your friends call you? Katy?"

"Yes, Katy."

"Then I'll call you Katy B."

Before the evening was over, I had regressed into a gushing teenager and I somehow knew that I would live the rest of my life with this man with a slight build and thinning red hair. His good manners and easy smile won my heart and I was convinced that fate had sent him.

Now he is everything to me. I shine my lights into every bush and flower bed, where now only pansies bloom—hoping to see my love, or hear a sound, a cry. But all I hear is the sound of the wind and then Mrs. Russell's chimes as I near her building. All I see is the darkness pierced by the beams of the flashlights. I call his name over and over. "Oz... Oz..." But there is no answer. Could he be hiding? I wonder.

Lights are coming at me. Relief. Someone else is out in

this dark night. As the headlights come closer, I see it is sheriff Billy. I almost faint with relief.

"Miss Kathryn, what are you doing out here in the freezing cold? Don't you know you'll catch your death?"

"It's Oz," I tell him. "He's missing. Please help me."

"Now Miss Kathryn, he'll be around. Let's get you inside before you catch pneumonia. Come on, get in the car. Let me take you home." He opens the passenger door. "And where's your coat? Don't you know it's winter out here?"

I stubbornly walk away.

He throws open the driver's door and gets out of the car, the motor still running, lights on. He stomps after me, grabs my arm.

"Now, Miss Kathryn, you come on back. You'll freeze out here. I'll call Donald."

"I don't want Donald. I want Oz. Don't try to appease me with his son. Just help me find Oz."

"Okay. I'll take you home and I'll look for him."

"You promise?"

"Don't I always, Miss Kathryn? Have I ever let you down?"

I sit in Oz's blue plaid easy chair near the back door. I sit alone in the darkness and wait. One thing I know for sure. Soon the sun will rise and burst into the kitchen window. Another day will begin. And this—this is all I know.

Rose-Colored Glasses

By Beverly Williams

When William took the midnight blue velvet box out of his pocket, Pamela squealed with delight. But her face fell when he opened the box and placed the ring on her finger.

"Don't you like it?" he said. "The jeweler said it was a very nice stone."

"It's sweet," said Pamela. "It's just … I thought it would be larger." She appeared so disappointed, almost on the verge of tears.

So William took the ring back and bought one with a larger diamond. It was more than he had planned to spend, but it made her happy, which was what he wanted. A ring is very important to a woman, he rationalized. The notion that a woman such as Pamela wanted him at all was so overwhelming he wasn't willing to let the smallest seed of doubt creep into his mind.

The wedding itself was not lavish, which William felt was fortunate, since he had to pay for it. Pamela was from England and her mother was too ill to come to Atlanta for the wedding. Her father had been killed in a fall from a polo horse years earlier. Pamela told him that the family's considerable fortune had dwindled over the years, but that they were still accepted by the royals. William was quite impressed by her first-hand knowledge of the royal family.

"Diana was a love," she said, "but Charles is a bit of an ass." No matter what she said, with that accent it sounded profound.

They moved into William's apartment and Pamela surprised him by immediately quitting her job. William had pictured them kissing each other goodbye as they went off to work in the morning, but Pamela said she wasn't making any money anyway and she needed to focus all her energy on making him happy.

She wasn't much of a cook, or perhaps William's tastes just weren't attuned to English food, and her decorating touches were a bit disjointed. William gave her a Visa card, and odd things began appearing in the apartment. A pair of fake fur pillows, one leopard and one zebra, turned up on the couch. She bought a lava lamp she saw in the window of an antique store that specialized in fifties merchandise. She took down a mirror that had belonged to his grandmother and replaced it with an ornate gilt-framed one. When William protested, she pouted, and he gave in. He stored his grandmother's mirror in the back of his closet.

But she certainly made him happy in bed. Every night and extra on the weekend. The frequency alone would have been enough to thrill William. He had been as close to a virgin as a thirty-four year old man could be, with only a few, mostly ill-fated, encounters to show for his attempts at female relationships.

By the time he met Pamela, he'd almost given up on ever finding a woman who would love him. He had concentrated on his work, and he had to admit it had paid off. He knew he was a tortoise sort of man, plodding along at a steady pace. But he was efficient and fair to his co-workers, and he had regularly been promoted. Not big dramatic promotions, but not lateral moves, either. He was steadily inching up the ladder, with raises in salary every time.

With each raise, he bought stock in his company. Now he was starting to diversify, because he knew a wise investor (he was beginning to think of himself that way) doesn't put all his eggs in one basket. Pamela didn't know about his investments. Not because they were a secret exactly, but William was a private person. He intended to tell her at some point. Surprise her with his astuteness.

"Why don't we go to England?" he said, when he got a bonus for the efficiency of his department. He had thought about buying a new bond issue, but was feeling a bit guilty about his secret investments.

"Oh, not now," she said. "This can be a beastly time of year in London. Maybe Mummy can come here for a visit. I'll ring her."

Hardly before William realized it, phone calls had taken place and arrangements had been made. He paid for Pamela's mother's plane ticket, since Pamela explained that, although the family had a large estate, there was little cash available.

Pamela's mother wasn't what William had envisioned. He'd pictured someone rather upper-crust dowdy, like the queen. Maggie was full-figured and blowsy, with a flirtatiousness manner that made William uncomfortable but seemed to bother Pamela not at all. They acted more like sisters than mother and daughter.

Maggie settled into the guest room like a bird making a nest. The apartment had only one bathroom, however, and it was a bit disconcerting to find Maggie's colorful lingerie dripping from the shower rod when he went in to take his morning shower. In order to close the shower curtain, William had to transfer Maggie's underwear to a towel rack. It was embarrassing to be handling his mother-in-law's bras and panties, like he was some sort of pervert, but he didn't know what else to do.

After two weeks, William began to wonder when Maggie was going back to England. He broached the subject with Pamela, but she cried and said she had been so lonely without her mummy, so William backed off.

"Just another fortnight," she whispered, in her charming accent. "Then we'll be alone again." She pacified him with silent but truly magnificent sex.

Then one day William came home from work to find the two of them drinking gin and tonics and poring over a stack of brochures.

"Darling!" Pamela exclaimed, jumping up to greet him with a kiss. William thought how fortunate he was to have such a loving wife. He remembered the days when he came home to a lonely apartment.

"How about a G and T, luv?" said Maggie. She gave him a pat on the rear, a habit she had which William considered highly inappropriate. He wished his precious Pamela had a more dignified mother.

"No, thanks," he said. He went in the kitchen and got a light beer from the refrigerator. He noticed the gin bottle was almost empty.

"Guess what, darling!" said Pamela when he returned to the living room. "Mummy and I have spent the entire day looking at houses."

"Houses? Whatever for?" William had begun to adopt Pamela's speech patterns.

"For us, silly boy. To live in."

"That's a bit premature, don't you think, sweetheart? I

hadn't planned on buying a house for two more years." He had a goal set for his portfolio. When he reached a certain amount, it would be time to invest in a house.

"But darling, this little flat is getting so crowded. And I worry about the crime, being so close to the city. The real estate agent says this is the perfect time to buy a house."

"The perfect time to buy a house is when we can afford it."

"But it doesn't cost anything to look. She says she will show us some houses this weekend. I just want you to see them."

"Pamela, we cannot buy a house now. And that's final." Hal, a friend of his at work, had said that you had to be firm with women, put your foot down when necessary.

"Scuse me," said Maggie. "I have to go to the loo."

Pamela scooted closer to him on the couch. "Please, darling." She licked his ear with her warm little tongue. "Just look. For me." William knew he would give in.

That weekend he went with Pamela and Maggie to look at houses. Within a week they had found the perfect house. It was in an older section of Atlanta that was becoming quite trendy, and William had to admit it appeared to be a good investment. Maggie stayed on to help with the move.

She stayed a bit longer to help them get settled. But at least in the new house her bedroom was not as close to theirs and she had her own bathroom, so her undies no longer hung from their shower rod. Nevertheless, William was looking forward to her departure. She had already stayed a month, so it couldn't be much longer.

Then one day he came home from work to hear the sound of laughter coming from the kitchen.

"Darling," said Pamela, flying into his arms as usual. "We have the most wonderful surprise. Look who's here."

Sitting at the kitchen table, gin and tonic in hand, was a strange man. About William's age, with a ruddy complexion and slightly thinning hair.

"It's Trevor," said Pamela, with such pride you might have thought it was Prince Charles. Maggie beamed. Pamela had told him about her brother who worked for the BBC. A producer, she said.

"Greetings, old chap," said Trevor, rising to shake William's hand. His voice was mellifluous, as befitted the BBC. William was impressed.

"Trevor had to come to Atlanta on business," said Pamela. "He decided to surprise us."

"He always was a scamp," Maggie said fondly.

"Well, this is wonderful," said William, recovering. "We're delighted to have you."

"I missed my little sister," said Trevor, giving Pamela a hug, "and Mummy, too, of course."

William thought it odd to hear a grown man call his mother 'Mummy.' But the English were different, as he was learning every day.

"How long are you going to be in town?" William asked. Maybe when he left, he would take Maggie with him.

"Not precisely sure," said Trevor. "I have business at CNN, and I'm doing some research on your Civil War. For a special we're doing on the BBC."

"I'm a Civil War buff myself," said William. "My great-grandfather on my mother's side was a Confederate colonel. There are some fantastic historic sites around here I can show you." He was beginning to become excited about Trevor's visit.

"That's a capital idea, old boy," said Trevor. He mixed himself another gin and tonic.

"Why don't you stay here with us?" said William. "There's

no need to go a hotel when we have plenty of room." Pamela and Maggie had just bought a sofa bed for the extra bedroom, the one that would eventually be a baby's room.

"Well ..." said Trevor.

"Oh, Trev, you must," said Pamela.

"What a smashing idea, William," said Maggie. "I hardly ever see him when we're in London. He works so much."

"There's a MARTA stop within a block," said William. "Goes right downtown to the CNN offices."

"How can I refuse?" said Trevor. "Thanks, old chap. And to celebrate, I'm taking everyone to dinner."

They went to a downtown restaurant that specialized in Southern food. William suggested it on the pretense of introducing Trevor to the local cuisine, but in truth he was becoming weary of Pamela and Maggie's cooking. Trevor picked up the check with a flourish and overtipped the waitress.

The next morning, William was fixing his toast and drinking his coffee when Trevor stumbled into the kitchen in his underwear. Jockey shorts. William hoped Trevor didn't go around in that state of undress in front of his mother and sister. William himself came from a proper, robe-wearing family.

"I wrote down the directions for getting to CNN on the MARTA," he said. He handed the piece of paper to Trevor.

"Oh, yeah, thanks, old man." He opened the refrigerator door and found a carton of orange juice. He poured a large glass, splashed in some gin, and downed it. "Ahhh. Hair of the dog, you know," he said cheerfully.

"Well," said William, a bit taken aback, "have a good day." He brushed his teeth, kissed a sleeping Pamela goodbye, and left for his office.

When he came home that afternoon, the scene was much

the same as before. Pamela and Maggie and Trevor were drinking and playing gin rummy. Pamela jumped up and kissed him as usual, although William thought it seemed a bit perfunctory. But perhaps that was his imagination.

"How was your meeting at CNN?" he asked Trevor.

"Oh, that's not till Monday. I need the weekend to get over the jet lag."

"Of course," said William. He had never flown far enough to get jet lag. "Maybe we can visit some Civil War battlefields tomorrow. Get you started on your research. I've been wanting to show them to Pamela."

"Oh, darling, I'm sorry. Mummy and I are going shopping. It's getting so hot here, and I don't have a thing to wear."

"Can't you go next week? This is very interesting. And educational." William had recently become aware of Pamela's lack of intellectual curiosity, something he'd hardly noticed before. And how she never even read the newspaper. Or anything else, except People magazine. He felt all she needed was for someone to open up new worlds to her.

"Rich's is having a huge sale. It's just for one day. I'll go with you next time, I promise."

William doubted it. The cynical thought surprised him, since he was not a cynical person by nature.

He and Trevor had a good time visiting Civil War sites. William had been interested in the war almost his whole life, and he loved having an audience to listen to his knowledge. Trevor didn't seem quite as interested as William would have thought a person doing research would be. He didn't make any notes or even ask any questions. When they arrived home, the living room was strewn with boxes and packages. Pamela and Maggie were both trying on clothes and sipping from the ubiquitous gin and tonics.

"We had the most marvelous time," enthused Pamela. "The prices were rock bottom. I bought Mummy a couple of things, too, since she really had nothing to wear in Hotlanta. I knew you wouldn't mind." She gave him one of the beguiling looks that had so captivated him when he first met her. Wide eyes like an innocent child, with the half-smile of an experienced woman.

"Of course," said William, although he was beginning to feel that Maggie took advantage of Pamela's generous nature. He was going to have to have a talk with her. Pamela, not Maggie. He had no intention of being alone with his vampish mother-in-law.

William mowed the lawn on Sunday afternoon while Pamela and Maggie went to the Peachtree Mall. "Just to look," promised Pamela. Trevor was still in bed, apparently recovering from his excesses of the previous night.

On Monday morning, Trevor had a nine o'clock business meeting at CNN. William left the car with Pamela, who said she needed to shop for drapery fabric, and he and Trevor rode the MARTA to downtown Atlanta. William walked the five blocks from the train stop to his office. He ought to do that every day, he thought, so he could leave the car with Pamela. He supposed he was going to have to get her a car of her own, but his Toyota was less than a year old and he hated the thought of two car payments. If she hadn't quit work, he thought ... she'd certainly been making enough for a car payment.

When he called to tell Pamela he had a meeting and would be late coming home (he always did that), there was no answer. Which meant she wasn't there cooking dinner and they'd be having pizza again. Ever since Maggie had arrived, Pamela had given her wifely duties short shrift. Mother or not, that woman was a bad influence. It was time she went home. He was definitely going to put his foot down this time. Even if Pamela cried, he'd be firm. He was the man of the house, after all, and enough was enough.

It was getting dark when he arrived home, but the car wasn't in the driveway. The surge of annoyance William felt was immediately replaced with a feeling of panic. What if they'd had a wreck? What if his precious Pamela was lying on a street somewhere, covered in blood? He ran the rest of the way to the house and burst through the front door, panting.

"Pamela! Pamela! Where are you, sweetheart?"

He flew from room to room, turning on lights, looking everywhere. The house was strangely quiet and still, with an unusual empty feeling. He tried to calm himself, fighting off the sense of foreboding that was creeping up on him. No need to panic, he told himself. It's not as if it were midnight. They're just out shopping. That's what women do.

Then he noticed that the lava lamp was gone. Maybe Pamela had finally realized what a monstrosity it was and gotten rid of it. He laughed, a weak little chuckle which sounded hollow in the room.

He checked the kitchen for a note and the answering machine to see if she had left him a message, but there was only his call to her, telling her he'd be late. He paced the floor, wondering if he should call the police. But they'd think he was silly, reporting a missing woman who was probably just shopping. Ridiculous. He got a Miller Lite from the fridge and paced some more, looking out the window every five seconds, expecting to see the car turn in the drive. What if they'd been carjacked? The crime was so bad in this city. Oh, God! They'd probably be killed, two women alone.

And where was Trevor? Was he with them? Surely he wouldn't still be at CNN. If he was with them, maybe they

would be safe, although Trevor didn't seem to be the protective type. Would he be brave enough to stand up to a car-
jacker? William was in agony. He wished he had a close
friend he could call, someone who would chuckle and say,
"For Pete's sake, man, they're just shopping. My wife would
stay at the mall all night if they didn't close."

By eleven o'clock, when they still hadn't arrived, he
turned on the television to see if they were reporting any terrible automobile accidents. During the national news and
the weather report, he called the emergency rooms of all the
major hospitals. He was becoming frustrated with the local
news. All they were reporting was hot weather, murders and
crime, standard summertime fare in Atlanta. Another bank
robbery this afternoon. Big deal.

As he was popping another beer, there was a pounding
on the front door. His heart almost stopped. Pamela would
use her key. It had to be news. He raced to the door, afraid
to open it, dreading to hear that she was hurt, maybe dead.
Oh, God, oh God, oh God, he whispered to himself. *Please
don't let her be dead.*

The pounding continued as he fumbled with the lock.
"I'm here," he said, his voice impatient but weak.

Two plain-clothes police stood on his doorstep, flashing
their badges. A uniformed cop stood behind them.

"William Potts?" the fierce-looking older one barked.

William nodded. He would have thought the police
would be more sympathetic when they were delivering bad
news.

"You own a dark blue Toyota Camry?"

William closed his eyes, in a mixture of relief and fear.
Oh, God, it was an automobile accident. Please, God, let
them tell him Maggie was the one who'd been killed. Let his
darling Pamela be alive.

"Was your car stolen?"

"Certainly not," said William. "My wife was driving it. What's this about?"

"Let's take a look, Simmons," said the fierce one to the uniformed cop. They shoved past William and started going through the house, guns drawn.

William started to protest, but the other plain clothes cop restrained him.

"We've got a warrant," he said.

"A warrant?" said William. "What's going on here?" Panic rose from his stomach to his chest. "Where's my wife?"

The cop ignored him.

"Nothing here," said the other one, returning. "He probably knows something. Let's take him down."

"You'll have to come with us, Mr. Potts."

One of them grabbed him roughly by the arm and steered him out the door. When William tried to jerk away, they slapped a pair of handcuffs on him.

"What do you think you're doing, Goddamnit?" screamed William, who never swore. "I want to know what's happened to my wife."

Neighbors' lights came on as they shoved William into the back of a squad car, pushing his head down in the process. He struggled for calm.

"I am a law-abiding citizen," he informed them, lowering his voice to sound more authoritative. "I demand to know why you are treating me in this manner."

"The First National Bank was robbed this afternoon. A witness got the license plate number. The car is registered to you."

"You idiots! My wife has been carjacked! Why aren't you looking for the criminals instead of arresting me?"

"What does your wife look like, Mr. Potts?"

"She's about five-four, blonde, blue eyes."

"What was she wearing?"

"I don't know. I left the house early." William could hear his voice becoming high-pitched and weak again, as he imagined Pamela being raped and killed.

"Does she own a pair of white shorts and a red flowered blouse? And an Atlanta Braves baseball cap?"

"Yes." The new clothes she'd bought Saturday. And his hat.

"The bank robbers were two women and a man. One of the women fits your wife's description."

William felt as if he would faint.

"No! There's some kind of mixup here. The carjackers must have forced her." He remembered the Patty Hearst case.

"One of the women was called Maggie. Do you know anyone named Maggie?"

"My wife's mother," he said weakly.

"And what's your role in all this, Mr. Potts?"

"Nothing. I swear. And my wife had nothing to do with it, either. They must have been holding a gun on her. If you'll just find her, we'll get this all cleared up."

He was regaining control. It was all a horrible mistake. He wouldn't put a little nefarious activity past Maggie and possibly Trevor, too, but not his Pamela. He would get it all straightened out, send her relatives packing, and they would be happy again. Just the two of them.

When they got to the station, William demanded a lawyer, just in case. But he didn't know one, except the lawyer who'd handled the closing on their house and he didn't want to call him in the middle of the night. The police took off the handcuffs and left him in a small room by himself. After about an hour, one of them came back in.

"We caught them. At least the Florida police did. They'd ditched your car and were in a bus station in St. Petersburg."

"What about my wife? Is she all right?"

"She's not hurt, if that's what you mean. But she's in a whole lot of trouble."

"Just get her back here. We'll get all this cleared up."

He tried to sound confident, but he was beginning to feel doubt. Could it be possible? He remembered yesterday when he came in from mowing the yard. Trevor and Pamela had been standing in the kitchen, heads together, laughing in an intimate way. He had seen Trevor give Pamela a very familiar pat on her shapely bottom. He'd tamped down his flair of proprietary anger. He could not imagine patting his own sister on the rear, but he decided that Pamela's family was just very different from his.

They released William on his own recognizance, though without a single word of apology for the indignities he'd suffered at their hands.

When Pamela, Maggie and Trevor arrived at the precinct in downtown Atlanta, he was waiting.

"Darling," he said, as Pamela was led past in handcuffs. The plaintive look in her eyes almost broke his heart. He persuaded the detective in charge to let him speak to Pamela alone.

"They made me do it," said Pamela.

"Your own mother? And your brother?"

"Maggie's not really my mother." Pamela didn't look him in the eye.

"And Trevor? What about him?" William remembered the familiar laughter and the pat on the bottom.

"Oh, Trevor," said Pamela dismissively. "He used to be my boyfriend, but that was ages ago."

"Pamela," said William sternly, "you are in a lot of trouble. I can't help you unless you tell me the truth. Everything."

"William," said Pamela, her voice a whisper, "I didn't really love you when we got married. I did it so I could stay in America. And Maggie wanted to come over, too, and then Trev. They were the ones who decided about the bank, and they blackmailed me. You see, I got in a tiny bit of trouble back home, and they said they would tell you all about it, and tell you I married you so I could stay here."

Pamela finally looked up at him. Tears swam in her big blue eyes.

"I begged them not to do it, darling, but they wouldn't listen to me, and I had no choice. I had fallen in love with you. I knew you would send me away if you found out and I just couldn't bear that. Trevor said he had the perfect plan, and he and Maggie would leave as soon as they got the money. All I did was watch the door. I swear."

"You've lied to me all along, Pamela. How can you expect me to believe you now?"

"But it's the truth. They said if I dropped them off at the MARTA stop, they would go straight to the airport and catch a plane back to England. I could go home and no one would ever know. I wasn't even going to keep any of the money, except a tiny bit for expenses. But then Trevor decided the police might check the Atlanta airport first and that it would be better to drive to Florida and go from there. I begged them to let me go home, but they needed someone used to driving on the right." The tears began anew. "I couldn't stand the thought of losing you, sweetheart. I did it for us."

William desperately wanted to gather her into his arms, kiss away her tears and tell her he would hire the best lawyer in Atlanta, one who could get her off on probation. He wanted everything to be like it was, to have his precious

Pamela back and the horrible intruders in jail, gone forever. He knew Pamela would show her gratitude in wondrous ways.

But William had lived a lifetime in the past twenty-four hours. The rose-colored glasses he had been wearing were stripped away. He was seeing clearly now. If he could believe she loved him, it would be different. But fantasy was no longer possible. Pamela did not love him and no amount of wishing could change it. She never had and she never would.

He looked at her tear-streaked face and shook his head regretfully. The pain of missing her was there already.

"Sorry, luv," he said, kissing her cheek, "you're on your own."

-⊰⊱-

How I Got into Show Business

By Nina Salley Hepburn

Daddy could always get up a crowd. Folks around Piney Grove still talk about how he started preaching when he was so little he had to stand in a chair to reach the pulpit. Men wearing shirts and ties, women in flowered dresses and children dressed in homemade hand-me-downs came from all over the countryside to hear the so-called boy wonder preach the gospel. At least, that's the story I've heard all my life.

Nothing stays the same though. By the time he got to be a teenager, Daddy had lost interest in preaching and saving souls. Show business beckoned him. He got a big western hat, some cowboy boots, a used guitar and taught himself to play and sing his favorite country songs. They say he was every bit as good as Hank Williams or Roy Acuff. He sounded like an ordinary hillbilly to me, but he could sure get up a crowd.

Mama and Daddy and all us kids would pile up in the old blue Ford station wagon and take off for a country fair or tent show. Daddy set up wherever he could find a stage and an audience. Soon as he grabbed the mike and let loose of a few bars of "Walking the Floor Over You," the crowd would start to gather. He was a born entertainer, no doubt about it.

"Sam Cullen sure can play the guitar and sing," people would say. "If he didn't have to run that farm, he could be famous, maybe even play at the Grand Ole Opry."

But he did have the farm to run. There were cows to milk and cotton to chop and plowing to do and I don't know what all else. He seemed to be working all day long.

That's the way things went until I was twelve. I was the oldest and Mama kept having more babies. About every year or two, there was a new one. I always had to help her take care of the little ones. Sue Nell was only 2 years younger than me, but she didn't have to do anything. Just sat around with her nose in a book all the time. Mama said Sue Nell was a born genius. "She'll go to college and be a doctor or lawyer—something like that and then take care of all of us." That was Mama's dream.

So of course we had to leave her to her books. Josephine—that was me—was made for taking care of babies and sweeping floors and helping with the wash. Stuff like that. If that wasn't bad enough, Sue Nell was pretty. Even if I hadn't had enough sense to see it for myself, people were always telling her how pretty she was. And Billy Joe was cute as a button, Katie was a perfect little doll, Lucy Ann was such a sweet child. Josephine sure was a big help.

That's how it was. Daddy getting up crowds, Mama having babies, all them getting some kind of attention. And me. I was just like an old work horse that hardly got any notice. I did have even teeth though. I heard somebody say to Mama, "Josephine has such nice straight teeth." It was a good thing for me, 'cause I knew there was no money for braces if I was to need them. I complained about being the only one who had to help her and the only one who wasn't pretty.

"But you have such nice teeth," Mama said.

"Who cares about nice teeth? I want to be pretty like Sue Nell and smart like her too."

"Well, you are smart," she said, "and you are getting pretty. Why just yesterday, I was telling your aunt Jane that before we know it, the boys are going to be chasing after you."

"Ugh!" I didn't like boys one bit and I sure didn't want them chasing after me.

"Just wait—before long, you'll be wanting the boys to notice you."

No way, I thought. But I didn't know much about human nature. And I didn't know about Daddy's next venture.

Just about the time school was out for the summer he found a new way to get up a crowd. He met a man called Willie Moon one night at a tent show. Our lives were about to change.

"Sam Cullen, you ought to be in show business," Willie said. "And I'm just the fellow that can help you get into it."

Before the night was over, they had made a deal and shook on it, as Daddy said. The very next day, Daddy told Mama he needed me to go help him get his new equipment. He was going into the motion picture business. Mama didn't like being left without me to help but Daddy told her I was the only one strong enough to help with the lifting.

This was some different kind of show business, I thought.

"She's got muscles like a boy," he said. Well, I just loved hearing that—when I was about to blossom out and be a girl!

"Come on, Josephine." So we hit the road, as Daddy would say, in the station wagon and drove in a straight line without stopping or turning, for about an hour before we came to a gravel road that had a hand-painted sign sticking up beside it. The sign read *Moon's Roadhouse*. An arrow pointed the way. Daddy hit the brake and the car screeched to a stop. He whipped the steering wheel around, the car rattling like nothing I ever heard. Then, like it jumped out from a dust cloud, a big red barn of a building appeared. There was a row of cars and trucks parked in the front. Daddy pulled the car in beside an old pick up truck and motioned for me to get out.

It was cool inside and pitch dark. The cigarette smoke was thicker'n the dust we'd just been through and between that and the dark, I couldn't see a thing 'til my eyes adjusted. Over at the bar there was a lot of loud talking and laughing going on, but when the men saw me, they kind of got quiet. Willie Moon came swaggering up looking like some kind of ole timey gangster in a pin-striped suit with a big fat cigar hanging out of his mouth. He and Daddy shook again.

"Stuff's out here in the back," Willie said and pointed toward a double door. Daddy shoved me ahead and I followed Willie Moon.

The room in back was bright. There may have been a window in it, but I'm not sure. There was a boy about sixteen or seventeen with blonde curly hair hanging loose around his face sitting at a table playing cards by himself. "This here's my nephew, Dean Harper," Willie Moon said. "He's gonna help you." The blonde boy stood up and he and Daddy shook.

"That's my girl Josephine," Daddy said. Dean Harper dropped his head and didn't even look at me. I didn't want to look at him either, but he was almost as tall as Daddy and had broad shoulders like a football player. He looked like a movie star if there ever was one. I couldn't help myself. Remembering my straight teeth, I smiled at him. Then he smiled and looked right at my teeth. I got this funny feeling inside that I had never had before. Could Mother be right?

Did I want a boy to notice me?

Here was the deal. Willie Moon was selling out. The sale included everything needed to run two movies in two different places, as well as two pop corn machines. Willie had a whole list of school buildings signed up, enough to run two shows every night of the week—except Sunday. Part of the deal was Dean. Daddy would go get him and drop him off, along with one projector, one screen, one speaker, one pop corn popper and the film reels for one show. Then Daddy would go on down the road to the other school and do the same thing. Every night of the week there would be different schools. It was quite exciting thinking about these picture shows being sent to us in Piney Grove all the way from Hollywood.

"It don't matter what you show," Willie said, "they'll just come a'flocking. It's the only entertainment they get for the whole week. Some will come right out of the fields, dirt and all. Others will be smelling of Aqua Velva and Cashmere Bouquet, all slicked up. They'll bring the whole family too. They'll pay two bits a piece and a nickel for the kids. You can sell lots of popcorn and cold drinks too. You can charge ten cents for those."

"Sounds good, Willie," Daddy said. "I sure hope I can make a go of it."

"No question about it," Willie said. He put his arm around Daddy's shoulder. "Sam, you're gonna be so rich, why you can give up farming before the year's up."

My head started whirling with all the thoughts. Being rich meant new clothes, a house in town and even a Cadillac car. But then, if it was such a good deal, why was Willie selling it to Daddy?

"Now you may wonder why ole Willie's letting go of such a money-maker," Willie said as if he was reading my mind.

"Well, Sam, I'll tell you. This here roadhouse is all one man can handle—even with Dean here to help. And a person can only spend so much money." He laughed and slapped Daddy on the back. "Besides, I like you. You're a talented fellow and I'd like to see you make a go of it."

I felt better about things and I guess Daddy felt good too. He shook Willie's hand and thanked him. "I'm much obliged you giving me this opportunity, Willie."

They started grabbing the equipment and heading for the car. As it turned out, I didn't have to use my big ole manly muscles. Daddy, Willie and Dean carried all the heavy stuff and loaded it in the station wagon. I did carry the precious picture show reels but they weren't too heavy. When Dean took them from me to put into the car, his hand touched mine. I got that crazy feeling again.

Driving home I thought about all the things we could buy with all that money. Mama wanted a new cook stove and new furniture for the living room. We could surely get that. And maybe a brick house like Aunt Jane's, with big columns and a porch, bedrooms for everybody and an extra bathroom. Daddy must have been thinking along the same lines because he barely said a word.

After we got home, we put on a picture show in our house. Mama made some popcorn on the stove and we sat on the floor eating out of a big bowl while we watched Tex Ritter ride across the faded wallpaper of our living room wall. *Sundown on the Prairie* was in black and white but it didn't matter. When it was over Daddy had one more surprise.

"Think I'll take Josephine with me this summer," he said. The film was rewinding on the projector and I was helping Mama clean up the spilled popcorn. "She can be a big help."

"It's bath time," Mama said. "Get the boys in the tub, Josephine." She grabbed up the bowls and marched into the kitchen, Daddy following behind.

I never knew what he said to her, but one thing was certain. Daddy was the boss in our family. And if he wanted me helping him, then that's the way it would be.

What an exciting summer this would be. Riding in the same car with Dean Harper night after night, watching movies every night of the week plus getting away from the babies and the dishes. Even if I had to carry heavy stuff, I didn't care. I'd sell tickets and popcorn and whatever Daddy needed me to do. The important thing was we were in Show Business and we were about to be rich.

The first night Daddy dropped me and Dean off at an old wooden school building at Curve—a tiny town named for the way the only road through town took a big bend and turned back on itself. People were lined up outside when we got there and had to wait while we got everything ready, but they didn't seem to care. They talked and laughed like they were real excited. And it was just like Willie Moon had said. Some were all dressed up like they might be going to church and others wore loose fitting overalls covered with farm dirt. Some of the women carried nursing babies and held the hands of little kids. Grandmas and Grandpas were lined up too, leaning on their canes.

Dean set up the projectors and speakers and sold tickets. I sold popcorn, candy and cold drinks. Folks eat and drink a lot when they're watching a picture show. My biggest job was making the popcorn. Over and over I filled the machine with corn, poured in the oil and when it had popped, stuffed it in the bags. That went on for an hour before the show started, while people crowded around yelling out their orders. I pulled the drinks from a big washtub full of chopped up ice. When Dean started the show, I could stand

up in back and watch *Sundown on the Prairie*—until inter-
mission when he changed reels. Then it was back to the
popcorn and drink station.

The picture show ended after a big shootout with the bad
guys. Tex got the pretty girl and they rode off into the sunset. The music came up and the credits rolled. Most everybody sat in their chairs until the reel wound all the way off
and Dean turned off the projector. I heard some of them tell
Dean how much they liked the show, promising to be back
next week.

As they filed out the door, we began our real chores—
putting everything away and cleaning up. A few bags of
warm popcorn were left in the machine and I handed them
to some little kids walking by. Then I cleaned up the popper
like Daddy had taught me. Dean wound up heavy black
electrical cords, then we both swept the floor that was lit-
tered with caked mud, popcorn bags and candy wrappers.

When Daddy came for us we'd be ready, with all the
equipment stacked by the front door.

"Well, Josephine, you're a good kid," Dean said as we finished up. "How old are you anyway?"

"Thirteen," I lied. Well, I would be in October.

"Is that all? I thought you were older." His superior look
made me blush.

I was about to lie again and say I was almost fourteen
when I heard the unmistakable honk of Daddy's horn.

By the end of the week I had memorized every scene of
Sundown on the Prairie and couldn't wait to get a new show.
Daddy paid Dean for the week's work but I don't know how
much. He gave me a brand new five dollar bill—more
money than I had ever had at one time. I was rich already.
And I was in love with Dean Harper.

Grandmothers on the Beach

By Beverly Williams

The beach house is quiet when I get up. I love the feeling of being the only one awake.

I slip into my most comfortable shorts, remembering when I used to wear tight cut-offs with frayed cuffs, so short they just barely skirted decency. These days, my shorts have elastic waists and are almost to my knees. Not bad, though, I think, as I look in the mirror. The legs are the last to go.

The living room is deserted, with remnants of last night's activity scattered about, like so much flotsam and jetsam. Damp beach towels draped on chairs. Potato chips now limp from the humidity. A bowl of those awful tortilla chips they all eat now—I think they taste like thin cardboard. Some kind of dip, dried and disgusting-looking. Drink glasses, Coke cans. I pick one up to throw it away. Almost full! The children are so wasteful these days, and the parents don't say a word. Of course, they are just as bad. And they wonder why they never seem to have enough money.

I do appreciate them bringing me along on this beach vacation, though. I paid for the rental of the house, which was exorbitant, but they drove us all down here in their monster van.

I let myself out the door and pick my way over the sand. The morning air is cool, with a breeze blowing off the ocean. It will be hot as Hades later. Way out on the horizon, there are a few shrimp boats and what looks like some kind of ocean-going vessel. They don't seem to be moving, although I'm sure they are.

Only a few people on the beach. A man with a little boy, trying to catch something in the surf. A healthy-looking older couple walking vigorously. Several dogs. I hope their owners are picking up after them. Probably not.

I take off my shoes and leave them on the wooden steps that go down to the beach, secure in the knowledge that they will be there when I return. Where I live in the city, they would be gone in a heartbeat.

Bare feet bring back memories of childhood and the sand between my toes makes me feel young. Not much does these days, so I take whatever I can get. It comes and goes. Some days I feel young, others like I'm a hundred. I just turned seventy-three, which is not all that old, though some might disagree.

I take off my hat, so I can feel the sun on my face and the breeze in my hair.

There are high-rise condos in the distance and I walk down to them, then turn and come back. Along the way, I meet other grandmothers on the beach, with their loose shirts and modest shorts, straw hats covering their gray or frosted blonde hair. We smile at each other in recognition. We were once the flat-stomached young girls in the tiny two-piece bathing suits, seeking quick tans on our Florida vacations.

When I return to the rented beach house, Camille, my oldest child, is up drinking coffee. She looks like she just rolled out of bed, hair sticking up, mascara smudges under her eyes. She is still wearing the thing she sleeps in, a huge tee shirt advertising some long-ago rock concert. Soon all the people who make nightgowns will go out of business. None of the younger generation, which is now getting older, wear anything but old tee shirts.

"Mother! Where have you been?" She sounds a bit grouchy, but then she never has been a morning person.

"Walking on the beach. It's a beautiful morning."

"I wish you wouldn't just disappear without telling anyone."

"Well, I don't know where else you think I'd be."

"I worry about you. At least leave a note next time."

"Okay." I think it's silly, but I'll do it. Anything to keep the peace. "Is anyone else awake?"

"Ken is stirring, but he'll lounge for another hour. The kids will sleep till noon. I don't know about the rest of them." Camille tightens her mouth in that way she does.

The 'rest of them' is my son Harrison and his new wife, along with his six-year-old son from his last marriage. They live in Alabama, so our visits are usually brief. This trip is an attempt at family togetherness, something that seems to have eluded us. I don't know if other families actually have it, or if they just sound like they do. Maybe we'll achieve it this time. We used to come here in years past, and I have been looking forward to this vacation ever since Camille first suggested it.

I've always loved this place. Years ago, I tried to get my husband to move here, but there was the business and the children's activities and we were settled in Memphis. When he retired, I brought it up again, but we were even more settled by then, and he never liked change, anyway. So we stayed where we were.

"So," I say, "what's on the agenda for today?"

Camille always has her days planned, punched into her Palm Pilot, which I think she loves more than her husband.

"Nothing," she says, surprising me. "I've been so stressed out, I just need time to relax and unwind. I am going to do absolutely nothing but lie on the beach and read. Ken and the kids can take care of themselves for a change."

Actually, Ken and the kids seem to take care of themselves most of the time. But I don't say anything. Since my children have grown up, I have become an expert at suppressing my opinion. Innocuous conversation is the order of the day.

"I do think you and I should have a talk," Camille says, putting on her clergy voice.

You wouldn't know it to look at her now, but Camille is an Episcopal priest, recently ordained. I am so very proud of her for achieving this, and still surprised, since there were times when I wondered if she'd ever be interested in anything but clothes and boys and parties. She was a wild teenager, while her brother was the straight one. Mister Goody-Goody, she used to call him.

"Let's talk now," I say. Get it out of the way. I pour myself a cup of coffee. It's too weak, but I don't want to criticize. I'll make some more later.

"All right." She agrees reluctantly, because she likes to set the agenda, which includes the time. She'd probably prefer to have her clerical collar on. I have to laugh to myself, the way she wears that collar all the time. I know she's proud of what she's achieved, and I am, too, but honestly. I just want to say, 'Give it a rest, honey.'

We take our coffee out onto the porch. There are more walkers down on the beach now.

"Well," I say brightly, taking charge, "what's on your

mind?"

As if I didn't know. I suspect now that this trip was planned to soften me up. Or to rally the family troops for an assault on me. Ever since my husband died a year ago, they've been trying to get me to move out of my house. As if widowhood immediately confers senility.

Camille pulls at the hem of her tee shirt, as if she can't assume her role as woman priest and senior child in such a scanty garment.

"I think it's time, Mother." Her voice is quietly dramatic. I have to give her credit, she knows how to play to an audience.

"Time for what?" I am taking the part of the cheerfully oblivious person, while in reality, I know I am being manipulated.

"Daddy's been gone for a year now. The estate is settled." Like I didn't know these things? "It's time for you to make some plans."

"Plans? What kind of plans?"

"I've been talking to Mindenwood Manor. Last week I went over there and toured the facility."

"Why in the world would you do that? You and Ken are too young for Mindenwood. And I don't think they'd let the children in." I chuckle at my little joke.

"Don't be ridiculous, Mother." Camille doesn't like it if you laugh when she's trying to have a serious discussion. "I think you should consider moving to Mindenwood. It's really lovely and it would be secure."

"And boring."

"No, it's not boring. They have lots of activities. They have speakers and they take the residents to plays and concerts. And there's a ladies' bridge club."

"You know I don't like bridge."

"Well, there's a mah jong group, too. And they even have aerobics. I think it would be great fun to live there."

"Then you go live there." I'm starting to get annoyed. Then I remember I have decided to be cheerful, so I throw in a smile.

"Mother, let's please have a serious discussion. You have no idea how I worry about you. Sometimes I wake up in the middle of the night, and I start thinking how someone might be breaking into your house. One night I got so panicked, I almost called you. At three a.m."

I smile to myself. God does grant justice, if you wait long enough. I cannot tell you how many nights I have lain in bed in a cold sweat, staring at the neon numbers on the bedside clock, waiting for Camille to come home. Do I have sympathy for her? Yes, but I still don't want to be manipulated into Dementia Manor.

Besides, I notice that her concern for my welfare has not motivated her to suggest that I come live with them. Not that I would, God forbid. All that frenzied activity, the loud music.

I have considered a retirement home, to be honest. They call it assisted living now, which means you start out in an apartment and as you become incapacitated, you move down the scale till you end up in the attached nursing home. I have friends who've made the move, though, and they seem fairly content.

And yet … somehow it goes against the grain. Like giving up. All my life I've been an optimist, looking forward to what is just around the corner, just over the next hill. That's the trouble with old age. The surprises are gone. When you're young, you look forward. It seems as if when you get old, you look back and wait for the inevitable.

But what if the inevitable doesn't come for another ten

or twenty years? What if I wasted all that delicious living time?

"I'll consider it, honey," I say. I don't want to talk about this any more; I just want to enjoy my time at the beach.

"I know what that means, Mother. You're just trying to get me to stop talking about it." My child knows me well. "It's time to do more than consider it. We need to start making some serious plans." She whips out the ever-present Palm Pilot. "Now, as soon as we get home, we'll put the house on the market. This is the best time of year to sell, you know. I've already talked to a Realtor. Betsy Westberry at Clarkson Brothers. She's one of my parishioners and she's very good."

"Well, I don't think there's any rush. After all ..."

She cuts me off. "Mother, you are not being fair. I cannot afford to spend any more sleepless nights. I have a busy schedule and I can't go around sleep deprived all the time."

The guilt trip. Not that I haven't used it myself. On occasion. But I don't feel guilty and I don't like the way she's steamrolling over me. I give her a disapproving look.

She softens.

"I know it's hard for you to think of giving up your house. It's a grief process, just like Daddy dying. But it's going to be so much better for you."

No, it's not.

"You'll have security and be around people your own age."

But I want to be around young people. Or at least people my own age who think they are young.

"And the apartments are just darling."

Darling? Ha! I've visited friends over there. The apartments are tiny, crammed with housefuls of furniture people can't bear to part with. And the bathrooms and kitchens don't even have a window. More depressing than darling.

"Ken agrees with me that this is the thing for you to do," she says. "And Harrison does, too." My son Harrison is so busy juggling his own life he can't even think about anyone else. He'll go along with whatever Camille says.

"Well," I say, "it seems that y'all have taken over my future. Such as it is."

"Now don't be that way, Mother. You know we want the best for you."

"I'm sure you do, honey." I smile. "I think I'll go get a shower. I have some shopping to do today." There's a huge outlet mall out on the highway where you can get wonderful bargains. Not that I need anything, but I do like to shop. And I want to get out and explore on my own.

An hour later, I've run the gamut of questions and slight disapproval and am driving Harrison's rental car down the highway. It's a convertible, and I try to feel free, to enjoy the ocean breeze through my hair. But the impending reality of the retirement home settles over me like a cloud. I suppose the children are right, that I should make the move. The house is much too large for me, and it is mighty lonely at night. If I should fall and break a hip (the ever present fear of the geriatric group), I could lie on the floor for hours, even days, before help arrived. And then I'd end up in a nursing home anyway.

When I arrive at the outlet mall, I'm surprised at the few cars in the parking lot. Then I realize none of the stores open until ten. It's only nine-thirty. So I get back in the car and drive. It's been years since I've been to this beach town, but I still know my way around. Lots of new high-rise condos on the beach and those mini-mansions that masquerade as beach houses, but on the side streets it's a different world. Like going back in time. Small frame or stucco houses with screen porches and flowers growing in the yards. People actually live here. I smell bacon and coffee, and I see a man watering his lawn. A kid on a bike. People going to work.

I turn a corner and see a house that makes me smile. It's a little pale green frame cottage with a screen porch across the front. It's not exactly rundown, but it has a comfortable shabbiness, as if it doesn't have to try so hard any more. Reminds me of myself. The grass has been mowed, but not edged. There are gorgeous red hibiscus growing in the front yard. They are probably perennial down here in this climate.

In front of the house there is a For Sale sign, with a Realtor's phone number on it. I stop the car. On the seat beside me is the cell phone my daughter insisted I bring with me. In case I got lost. Without thinking beyond the moment, I punch in the Realtor's number and push the send button.

By the time I arrive back at the beach house, they are all awake. The smell of suntan lotion overlays everything else. My son is in the kitchen mixing Bloody Marys.

"Hey, Mom," he says idly. "Where've you been?"

"Oh, just doing a little shopping."

"Camille's about to have a hissy fit. She thinks you've been kidnapped or something."

"Oh, for heaven's sake," I mutter. "I'm fine. Just because I didn't check in every hour."

"You know how she is," says Harrison. He fills a cooler with ice and picks up the pitcher of Bloody Marys. "Gotta go, Mom. Everyone's waiting on these. Why don't you come on down to the beach?"

"Maybe in a little while."

"Okay. I'll tell Camille you're back, so she can stop praying." He grins at me.

I want to talk to Harrison, but he never has time. Still, I

think there's a chance he might be on my side.

I pour a Bloody Mary and drink a silent toast to myself. Then I fix a tuna sandwich and sit out on the porch and read. I hear voices floating up from the beach. It's very pleasant. I'm dozing in the chaise longue when a voice startles me awake.

"Honestly, Mother, you could have called. I was worried sick."

"I was fine, Camille."

"You were gone for hours. I kept calling you on the cell phone and you never answered."

"I left it in the car. When I was shopping." Apparently this is not a satisfactory explanation, because I can tell she is still miffed.

But I don't care. I have made a decision and done something about it. Just when I thought there were no new adventures around the corner. I am dying to tell someone, and I wish it could be my children. It was impulsive, I know, but I don't have time to be thoughtful and prudent. And I don't want to, anyway.

I am going to lay low for the rest of this vacation, not stirring up suspicions. I feel badly about deceiving my children, but I can't afford to let them know about my plans until we're safely back home. Then I will tell them I have bought the little green house. Instead of shuffling into Mindenwood Manor and drying up and dying, I am moving to Florida and starting a whole new life.

All of a sudden, the years have fallen away. I am excited, looking forward to each new day and to what's around the next corner. I am young again.

About the Authors

Nina Salley Hepburn

Nina Salley Hepburn has won awards for her fiction and poetry. Her profiles and other articles have appeared in several regional publications, including *Memphis* magazine. She formerly edited a monthly newspaper, *The Memphis Pages*. She and her husband, David, live in Germantown, Tennessee, and Sarasota, Florida.

Beverly Williams

Beverly Williams is a born and bred Southerner who grew up listening to family stories and eavesdropping on front porch gossip. She has been writing for most of her life. She lives in Memphis with her husband, Duncan, and chocolate lab, Sally.